# A Rescued Heart

*To my reader —*
*with love*
*and appreciation —*

*Alene Roberts*

## Alene Roberts

Published and Distributed by:

Granite Publishing and Distribution, L.L.C.
868 North 1430 West • Orem, UT 84057
(801) 229-9023 • Toll Free (800) 574-5779
FAX (801) 229-1924

Second Printing; October 1999

Cover Art and Design by: Tamara Ingram
Page Layout and Design by: *SunRise Publishing, Orem, Utah*

ISBN: 1-890558-64-8
Library of Congress Catalog Card Number: 99-95474

# Acknowledgements

With deep gratitude, I acknowledge the many blessings I have received from my Father in Heaven. He gave me this book when I was seriously ill from deadly insect bites—to cheer me up, as well as, hopefully, *all* those who read it. Norman Rockwell said: "I didn't want to paint the evil in the world, I painted the way I would like life to be." In this troubled world, we occasionally need a moment of respite—finding a place and people whose lives lift us up, make us smile and make the world a better place.

Again I thank my son, Whitney Roberts and his wife, Lisa, who are always eager and ready to critique my writing, boosting my morale. Because of a suggestion Lisa gave me, I added another chapter, making it a better book.

I give a smiling thanks to my daughter, Cynthia Shaw and her four children, Morgan, Lauren, Catie and Michael. They read it together and gave me valuable input. And a special thanks to Lorrie Curriden, Cynthia's friend, a prolific reader, who took time out to read this. She too, gave me invaluable suggestions!

Thanks to my daughter, Christie Atkinson, who when I read parts of the still unfinished manuscript to her a couple of years ago, said: "That is going to be published, Mom," giving me a much needed boost in confidence. Thanks to her daughters—my granddaughters, Jamie and Leah who read the manuscript and told me they loved it.

To Elliott, my husband, I give my heartfelt thanks for staying by my side for hours helping me find errors and fine-tuning this story. I couldn't have done it without him!

Again, I am grateful to Granite Publishing and Distribution. Thanks to Jeff and Ron for their integrity and kindness. Their upbeat spirit always lifts my own. Thanks also to the other stalwarts at Granite: David, Joyce, Amy and Coreen.

# *Dedication*

To my grandchildren and all my posterity—
May a Fenn or a Dilly come into their lives at the appropriate time.

# *Chapter One*

"Where *is* that girl?" the bus driver muttered, glancing at the building across the street. The paunchy, middle-aged driver looked at his watch, noting that it was time for the bus to leave. He drummed his fingers against the steering wheel in frustration. Doggone that girl, he thought—in a moment of rash assertion—if she thinks I'm going to sit and wait for her every time—holding everybody up, she's got another think coming!

Five minutes later, still grumbling to himself, he looked into the right-view mirror for the perpetually late passenger then again checked his watch. Shaking his head in exasperation, he monitored the traffic through the left-view mirror, pulled out slightly and began driving slowly alongside the curb. Sure enough, there was the red hair bobbing up and down outside the windows, then she was at the doors, waving, smiling.

Stopping the bus, he glared at her, then opened the doors. Dilladora Dobson's long legs took the first two steps, easily and gracefully, then the third. Smiling and breathless, she showed her pass to the perturbed driver.

"Doggone it, Dilladora, you're going to get me fired or get yourself killed, or both."

"You worry too much, Joe."

"When you get another bodyguard, I..."

"No more bodyguards, Joe. I hope I'll never have to put up with another one of those annoying, muscle-bound gorillas following me around everywhere."

"Well," he said, glowering, "I hope you do!" He pulled the bus out into the street, picking up speed. "And I hope the next bodyguard will have enough of what it takes to keep you from running alongside the bus."

"Can I help it if I was a track star?"

Joe smiled in spite of himself. "The bus was so crowded when you got on earlier, I couldn't ask why you came to the Fashion Fare building on a Monday?"

"Oh, Bernie talked me into an extra session."

Joe heaved a sigh. "Why don't you buy a car, Dilladora, and quit riding the bus so I can have some peace?"

She gazed into the pleasant face of her favorite bus driver. "I've told you before, Joe, I don't want to worry with the upkeep of a car. Besides," she said, an impish but affectionate smile on her face, "you know I relieve the monotony of your days."

"Go sit down."

"Yes, sir!"

Walking down the aisle, her full, mid-calf skirt swaying with the movement of her hips, she found a seat. All male eyes were upon her, young and old, admiring. Nevertheless, at twenty-seven years old, Dilladora Dobson was past feeling flattered. Experience with men through the years had proven to her repeatedly that there was no one— like Uncle Obadiah. No one with his brains, no one with his understanding, his sense of humor, kindness, nor with his value system. Knowing that she could not marry less of a man, she reconciled herself to living the lonely life of a single. Though dating now and then to add a little zest to her life, she had no hope that a man with half the qualities of her 'Uncle Obi' would come into her life. The four years since his death seemed like an eternity to Dilladora. It was only recently that she realized, as her aunt Isadora often pointed out, she was idealizing him a little, but even so there was still no one like Uncle Obadiah.

Smiling, she settled back to enjoy the beautiful fifteen minute drive between Medford City and Bostonville. The lush oasis of citrus groves and vegetable farms on both sides of the highway, between the two cities, was due to the foresight of her great-grandfather Obadiah Penbroke the First. She always felt proud of this. The very wealthy Penbrokes hailed from Boston. Great-grandfather Obadiah and his wife Catherine, tired of the cold winters in Massachusetts, moved to the beautiful, warm, golden state of California.

A voice broke into her reverie. "Were you speaking to me?" Dilladora asked, turning to the woman next to her.

"Yes, I was," the woman said with a touch of asperity. "I asked if you were from Bostonville."

"Oh. Yes I am."

"I'm a reporter from the Los Angeles Times," the woman stated. "I was visiting friends in Medford City when I decided to do a piece on Bostonville and the eccentric old man who founded it." Her brows arched and a small smile appeared, "Maybe you can tell me something about him since he's somewhat of a legend in the city."

"I can," Dilladora said, more than eager to oblige. "I understand that Obadiah Penbroke the First and his wife, Catherine, were from Massachusetts. Apparently, Catherine became very homesick for Boston, so Obadiah bought thousands of acres and began building a city patterned after Boston and named it Bostonville. It became a city with its own mayor, own police force, newspaper, stores and even a small community college. Of course today, the college is a university called Bostontown University."

"Well," the woman interrupted, "that's very interesting, but I...uh" she leaned over and whispered, "would like to know if there's any scandal connected to the family. I understand the Penbrokes are very wealthy and control everything in Bostonville. Nobody can take a breath unless they get the okay from old lady Penbroke."

Dilladora flushed with irritation. "I can assure you that Bostonville is a city with very little crime and a lot of community spirit—which most people feel is due to the *influence* of the Penbroke family."

"Well, I've heard that no one can even buy property for development unless they get permission. Isn't that so?"

"If you mean," Dilladora began with an edge to her voice, "do they retain all the land around the city they have planted in citrus groves and vegetable farms? The answer is yes, but that is what makes Bostonville such a unique place. This protects the city from unseemly growth like most other California cities."

The woman sighed impatiently, "What I'm really trying to find out, young lady," the reporter looked around and lowered her voice, "is something about that niece of the Penbrokes. I hear she's really a 'wild hair,' always getting into scrapes of some kind or another."

Dilladora stifled an urge to laugh out loud. Instead, she feigned surprise and put on a pious demeanor. "Oh my no, I know her well. She's as docile as a lamb and goes around doing nothing but good works."

"Oh," the woman said, obviously disappointed. "Well, if you'll excuse me," she said, standing up and stepping over Dilladora, "this is my stop coming up. What did you say your name was? I may even mention you in the article."

"Oh you will? How nice," she said with sticky sweetness, "I'm Dilladora Dobson. I'm," she said, mimicking the reporter, "'old lady Penbroke's niece.'"

The woman opened her mouth but nothing came out; the light complexion of her face turned pink. Abruptly turning, she walked to the front of the bus, and without a backward glance, quickly stepped off.

Feeling justified, Dilladora smiled and leaned forward to watch the retreating woman. She sat back and sighed as she contemplated her Penbroke heritage, remembering ruefully when she once found it a burden.

After graduating from college, she decided to move to and work in Medford City where no one knew she was a Penbroke; a place where she could do her 'own thing' without it getting back to Aunt Isadora. Or so she thought. Her aunt, seeming to have an inexhaustible supply of informants, always found out one way or another and constantly begged her to come back home.

About two years ago, she realized her weekly visits home did not suffice. She was twenty-five, and lonely. Giving up her small apartment in Medford City, she moved back to the comfortable, familiar surroundings of the Penbroke family home.

She knew the pitfalls of living with her aunt, the most annoying of which were the bodyguards Aunt Isadora insisted on hiring after that silly kidnapping scare. To date, there had been nine body guards in all. Each, after only a couple of months, had managed, with Dilladora's help, to get himself fired. Hopeful that her aunt would finally give up on it, she continued to live at home. A whole month had passed since the last one and she found it a great relief to come and go without someone following her everywhere.

"Dilladora, your stop!" yelled the bus driver.

Startled, she jumped up and walked to the door. "Thanks, Joe." She smiled. "See you tomorrow."

"Not if I'm lucky you won't," he grimaced.

The bus stop was on the corner, two homes down from Aunt Isadora's old brownstone. Dilladora loved this street, Beacon Avenue. Great-grandfather named it after the famous Beacon Hill in Boston, even though each of the brownstones was different in design and shade of brick. They borrowed their different facades from the town homes on Walnut street in Philadelphia, from Beacon Hill in Boston, and the Georgetown row houses and the Queen Ann townhouses in Washington D.C. Her great grandparents chose the latter design with its bay windows and 'cut brick' exterior. All were alike in that they were wider than usual with small front yards to show off beautiful California foliage. The street, traveling several blocks up, was canopied by large old trees whose magnificent limbs also shaded the wide sidewalks. These homes were more stately than the Brownstones on Beacon Hill in Boston because of an extra high foundation, making it possible to have three steps up to the front porch. Beautiful potted plants and flowers graced each porch of this majestic upper-middle-class neighborhood.

Only two blocks over from Beacon Avenue, Bostonian-like mansions graced the city. Their elegantly landscaped yards each took up at least a half block; a neighborhood where Aunt Isadora and Uncle Obadiah could have lived. Instead, they chose to remain in Great-Grandfather Obadiah's original home.

Running up the steps, Dilladora opened the front door. The delicious smell of dinner in progress greeted her, bringing back nostalgic memories of coming home after school to Sophie and her cooking, and to Max, Sophie's husband, who served as the family gardener. It evoked memories of coming home to her beloved aunt and uncle who were more than that to Dilladora—they were parents.

Not wanting to run into her aunt until she freshened up, she closed the door quietly. She paused, hearing voices in the library. Across the expanse of the spacious foyer, the area split; the stairs on the right marched upward to the second floor. On the left a hallway ran in a straight line from front to back, ending at a door that led to the veranda. The wide double doors of the library, directly across from the stairs, were open. Maybe she could get upstairs without Aunt Isadora and guest noticing. An elegant light green rug, with floral designs in the corners and intermittently along the sides lay on the polished hardwood floor, muffling her steps as she walked quickly to the stairs. Halfway up, the strong voice of her aunt reached her.

"Dilly, you're home! Come and meet this young man."

Dilladora stopped her ascent. "Oh no," she muttered under her breath. She turned, leaning over the polished mahogany banister, she put on a bright smile and said, "Oh hello, Aunt Issy." Reluctantly, she descended the stairs, crossed the hall and entered the library. Leaning down, she kissed her aunt then straightened up and stared at the young man.

"Not another one, Aunt Issy," she groaned.

"Yes, another one, Dilly, and mind your manners. This is Dunley Fennimore Dinkle. Mr. Dinkle, this is my niece, Dilladora Dobson."

The young man stood up, took a step toward her, and nodded.

"Glad to meet you, Miss Dobson."

Dilladora stared up at him, realizing he must be at least eight inches taller than her five foot seven. *"Dunley...Fennimore...Dinkle?"* she repeated.

"Yes ma'am."

"Why, Aunt Issy—how very clever of you. The alliteration of the d's in our names—I can't believe it. How did you ever find him? He must be *the one*—just think—Dilly Dinkle. Why that's even sillier than Dilly Dobson," she said, looking pointedly at the newcomer. She noted that the young man didn't even bat an eye. A cool character, she thought.

Dunley Fennimore Dinkle did, however, cast a quick glance over at Isadora Penbroke and saw an expression of resigned exasperation.

Dilly Dobson looked the young man over. "He's different from the others, Aunt Issy. He's not a 'pretty boy.'" She walked around him, appraising him as one would appraise a prize bull at the state fair. "He seems a little on the slim side to be a bodyguard, Aunt Issy. No overly beefed-up muscles." Though she did notice that his broad shoulders and chest filled out his shirt nicely. "How old are you, Mr. Dinkle?"

"Thirty."

"Why aren't you married?"

"How do you know I'm not?"

"Because Aunt Issy never hires married men. As I asked before, why aren't you married?"

"Why aren't you?" he rejoined, unperturbed.

"Why he's downright sassy, Aunt Issy. Thirty and not married...hmm...what are you doing about your hormones, Mr. Dinkle?"

"Dilladora! Behave yourself." Isadora's exasperation, it was plain to see, was no longer resigned. "Please go upstairs and freshen up for dinner. It will be ready in thirty minutes."

"Yes, Aunt Issy." She smiled sweetly. "Nice to meet you, Mr. Dinkle." Turning gracefully, she flounced out of the library to the stairs, then taking three steps at a time, she disappeared.

Isadora turned her gaze toward the young man. "Please have a seat, Mr. Dinkle."

"Thank you."

"Well, do you think you can handle the job?"

"The price has gone up."

Isadora laughed. "I thought it might."

"If she's always this offensive, I can see why you're worried about her being bound, gagged and dumped into a well. I don't know if you can pay me enough to put up with her."

"Refresh my memory. What did you say you do besides managing the personnel at the training center, Mr. Dinkle?"

"I would be obliged if you would call me Fenn, short for Fennimore."

"Thank you, Fenn."

"I work as a journalist for the Medford City Times and the Bostonville Globe. I want to continue writing, but my main goal is to start a publishing house that specializes in a certain type of literature."

"Yes, and I believe you told me something else, that you had built up and sold a small software company."

"Yes."

Isadora tilted her head appraising him—then she smiled knowingly. "When you told me this before, I remember thinking that your 'casual, awe shucks' way of speaking didn't match your education and accomplishments."

Fenn just smiled, knowing she wanted an explanation but felt it was none of her business.

Isadora waited expectantly. The silence stretched out. Finally she asked a little impatiently, "is it a put on?"

"A put on? The way I speak?"

"Yes."

"What you see is what you get, Mrs. Penbroke."

"That isn't an answer, Fenn."

Irritated at her persistence, he blew out a quick breath. "I'm a casual person by nature so when I become a little erudite, I find I put people off—or they don't know what I'm talking about."

Isadora smiled. "Thank you, Fenn. Now about your ambitious goal—I have the connections and the money to get you on your way if you accept the job and do it well. You will also receive a salary of a thousand dollars a week."

"A thousand a week?" he gasped. "On second thought," he grinned, "maybe you *can* pay me enough to put up with her. You say that I'm to uh...follow her everywhere she goes...every day...all day?"

"Yes. And if she goes out in the evening, there will be evening work also."

"Sundays are out."

"That's fine. Dilly seems to rest from her labors on Sunday."

"And just what are her labors, may I ask?"

"She's on a one woman crusade."

"What is she crusading for or against?"

"You'll find out, if you remain on the job long enough, that is."

Dunley Fennimore Dinkle could not believe that he was sitting in this marvelous library, in this beautiful house, in this crazy situation and that he was even contemplating accepting the job. But could he afford not to? Crazy or not.

"Of course," Isadora broke into his thoughts, "you will have to sign a contract and if you break the agreement in any way, the contract will be null and void and you will be dismissed."

"How many bodyguards have you had before me?"

"More than I can remember."

"Did they quit, or did you dismiss them?"

"None of them quit. They liked the salary too well."

"Why did you dismiss them?"

"They all broke the contract."

Fenn Dinkle frowned, suddenly suspicious. "May I study the contract, Mrs. Penbroke?"

"You may. However, call me Isadora."

This request surprised Fenn. Isadora Penbroke, though always charming and friendly while at the training center, kept everyone at arms length with the formality of 'Mr. and Mrs.,' and expected the same from them.

"Yes ma'am. Thank you."

"We'll have dinner and then you may go over both the contract and the application."

Questions were swirling around in his head. Why would this woman spend so much money on such a seemingly spoiled and willful young woman who was, after all, only her niece?

He focused on the woman herself. Not as tall as her niece, but almost as slim, she appeared to be at least sixty. Her brown eyes were intelligent, alert and seemed to sparkle with a constant effervescent humor. High cheek bones, a prominent straight nose and an authoritative jaw gave her distinguished face a look of strength. Though her face was relatively free of wrinkles except around the corners of her eyes, gray was beginning to show at the roots of her lovely auburn-dyed hair. A multicolored scarf tied around her head, the ends trailing upon her left shoulder, matched the flamboyant colors of her long-sleeved silk blouse and slacks, over which a long filmy vest hung loosely. Someone else, he thought, wearing this conglomeration of colors and type of clothing, would look like a gypsy, but not Isadora Penbroke. She definitely lent the clothes a touch of class, sophistication and glamour.

A sturdily built woman appeared at the door of the library, wearing a blue cotton dress and a white apron. She appeared to be assessing the situation while Fenn assessed her rather uncommon face—large green eyes, full generous lips encased in an oblong face framed by short wiry blonde hair. The stranger in the library did not deter her.

"Dinner's on, Mrs. Penbroke," she announced in a commanding tone, "and if you don't come now, I'll throw it to the pigs." Before Isadora could respond, the woman turned, walked to the foot of the stairs and yelled. "Dillweed, dinner's on!"

Dilly Dobson came bounding down the stairs. "Yippee! I'm starved, Sophie." She gave the formidable woman a kiss on the cheek. A hint of a smile on her face, the woman called Sophie marched back in the direction from which she had come. Dilly turned her attention to the occupants of the library.

"You still here, '*Dudley*' Dinkle?" She entered the library. "Oh yes, that's right, Aunt Issy wants you to taste Sophie's scrumptious cooking—a further incentive for you to accept the job, as if I'm not incentive enough. And did she tell you that you also get free board and room? You'll just be one of our big happy family, won't he Aunt Issy?"

"You're being tiresome, Dilladora."

"Dilladora is quite an unusual name," Fenn remarked to the Aunt.

"Of course it is," stated the owner, smiling sweetly. "And when Aunt Issy calls me Dilladora, it means she's a little piqued at me."

"I think I heard someone call you Dillweed a moment ago," commented Fenn, his eyes twinkling.

"Ah yes, that's cook. She's chronically piqued at me. Actually, Dillweed is my favorite nickname. When I outran, out batted and out pitched all the little boys on the block, they nicknamed me Dillweed to get back at me. The male species are sore losers—even when they're little boys—that is, when they lose to a female."

Fenn smiled, ignoring the slight. He noted that Dilly Dobson who hadn't changed for dinner, was still in the odd color combination of a natural shirt, a sage vest and a long full forest green skirt. The ensemble was amazingly attractive, he decided, when combined with her shoulder length, slightly curled, copper-red hair.

Her large bright blue eyes were quite startling at first, then one noticed the creamy complexion and the nicely rounded cheek bones, tapering gently to a delicate but determined jaw line and chin. Under her patrician nose, her mouth with its full lower lip was shaped in such a way that she appeared always on the verge of a smile. He suspected that her smile would be beautiful if she ever decided to favor him with a sincere one. The total picture presented was one of casual glamour.

Dilladora, already annoyed over his lack of reaction, was now thoroughly irritated at his perusal of her. Turning on her heel and with a flip of the head, she clipped out of the library in the same direction that Sophie, the cook, had gone.

"She's quite a beauty, Mrs. Penbroke, I mean, Isadora."
"Yes, and she uses it to the hilt."
He smiled. "I suspect as much."
"Shall we proceed to the dining room, Fenn?"

~~~~~~~~~

Dinner turned out to be as "scrumptious" as Dilladora had promised. Fenn considered himself a connoisseur of good food. Raised by a mother who was a wonderful cook, she insisted that all her children learn to like everything. Sophie and her husband, Max, served the meal. It consisted of filet of sole baked in a delicious cream sauce, cooked peas, carrots with dill and baby leaf lettuce salad. All the vegetables were from Max's garden, Isadora informed him. Light, delicious, homemade rolls served with the meal, gave it the zing of Sunday best in Fenn's book. Blueberry pie, made from blueberries grown in Max's berry patch, finished it off to perfection. It was almost worth putting up with Dilladora Dobson just to eat the meals here, Fenn decided.

During the meal, the damsel in question chattered to Sophie and Max. Sophie only grunted or nodded and Max's blue eyes crinkled at the corners every time Dilly opened her mouth. In spite of his rolled up shirt sleeves and frayed jeans, Fenn thought Max would make a fit butler with his graying blonde hair, tall frame and polite, gentlemanly manner. However, his suntanned face and arms and large calloused hands revealed his work as an outdoor man.

Fenn guardedly watched Dilly Dobson eat, fascinated. In all his life he'd never seen a young woman eat as much. He wondered how she stayed so slim. Meanwhile, she totally ignored him, apparently bored by the whole affair—the wooing and dining of the potential new bodyguard who was just the latest of many.

After finishing her second piece of pie, Dilly jumped up, began piling up the soiled dishes, then walked out with a stack of them in her hands. Fenn looked over at Isadora, questioningly.

"Dilly loves Sophie and Max. She feels that they work too hard, so she helps them with the dishes every night."

"Well, what do you know."

Isadora chuckled. "Oh, Dilly does have a couple of redeeming qualities."

"I'm curious, Mrs. Penbroke, I mean, Isadora, I'm amazed that you would spend so much money on uh...a niece."

"I have raised that girl most of her life. Obadiah's silly, much younger sister, Lilly, was her mother. She was always getting into one ridiculous scrape after another, that is, after her husband died. Dilly was two when she lost her father. I finally convinced Lilly that it would be better for her daughter if they lived with us so she would have a father figure in her life. Dilly was four when they moved in. Well—we became her parents and Lilly became her 'once-in-a-while' mother. In this respect, it was not good for Lillian, but very good for Dilly. She adored Obadiah and he adored her. She's the child we wanted and couldn't have."

"I understand that you are a widow, Isadora. When did Mr. Penbroke pass away?"

Her face became thoughtful. "Four years ago, shortly after Dilly turned twenty-three. It was a terrible time for both of us. Dilly took it especially hard." She rose abruptly. "Come, Fenn, let me show you the living quarters, then we'll go back to the library and you can look over the contract."

Fenn stood up. "May I say, Isadora, that your home here is lovely."

"Thank you, Fenn. The first Obadiah Penbroke, the founder of Bostonville, built this home. In fact he was responsible for all of Beacon Ave."

"I've never been in a brownstone before," he said looking around, "I'm intrigued with how they're laid out."

"As you can see, Fenn, brownstones have common walls with the homes on either side, making it mandatory to use the light from the front and back windows. That is why they combined the dining room here with the front room."

"Yes," he said noticing the tall, wide bay window in the front with its crescent window on top. He also noticed that, like her clothing combinations, Isadora's home was eclectic—mixing vintage collectibles and Victorian antiques with comfortable modern day upholstery.

"Your decorating, Isadora, gives the old family home a distinctive look of class, as well as comfort."

"Why thank you, Fenn," she said, obviously pleased.

Isadora led him out of the room to the foyer. Fenn noticed, for the first time, the crescent window above the wide front door. The long, narrow, pastel-stained windows on each side shed a rainbow of muted light upon the Queen Ann writing table against the wall. The warm light also enriched the elegant walnut hall tree and brass umbrella holder on the left.

As they passed the library, Fenn remarked, "Obadiah Penbroke the First must have leaned more to study than to entertaining."

"Why do you say that, Fenn?" she asked, surprised.

"Because the library is much wider than the front room, and has two bay windows."

She smiled. "You're right, Fenn. He was a self-educated man."

Progressing down the wide hall, Isadora pointed to the bright, updated kitchen on the right behind the dining room. Across the hall from the kitchen, a sunny television room filled with cushioned wicker furniture caught his eye.

Fenn sucked in his breath as they stepped out onto the beautiful veranda filled with potted plants and flowers. Looking beyond to the yard, the size of it surprised him. "This is a much bigger backyard than I expected."

"It is, Fenn. When Obadiah's grandfather built this home, he was so taken with California's weather and fertile soil, he reserved extra land by extending our yard all the way through to the next street, then adding two lots on either side. So we have the equivalent of six lots including this one behind our home."

Fenn noticed that flower beds flanked both sides of the yard directly behind the house. Left center stood a magnificent old tree that mimicked the full red-leaf maples of the East. A white bench swing hung temptingly from one of its spreading, gnarled limbs.

"On the right of the veranda here," Isadora explained, "that vine-covered walkway leads to the garage. On the other side of it," she said, pointing to a lovely brick cottage, "is where Sophie and Max live."

"Your quarters are above the garage," she added, walking across the veranda to the covered walkway. Fenn followed her to the outside stairs that led up to the apartment.

The furnished apartment was a surprise to Fenn. Decorated in a tasteful masculine style, it consisted of a bedroom, a bath, a small kitchenette and a nice sized front room with a long leather couch and two large leather chairs. And, he noted with excitement, there was a built-in bookcase all along one wall.

Fenn sat in one of the chairs, gratified that it fit his long frame.

"Mighty comfortable up here, Isadora, mighty comfortable."

"I'm glad you like it, Fenn."

He got up and looked out the large window. From here he could see the whole yard. It looked to Fenn to be at least three-quarters of an acre. Walking paths meandered around a Monterey pine, an olive tree and several citrus and led invitingly to a grape arbor, then to a berry patch and a vegetable garden.

"The window gives you a good view of the grounds and veranda where Dilly might entertain a friend or friends," Isadora commented.

"Seems a bit like spying to me."

"You misunderstand, Fenn, it's not Dilly I don't trust, it's her friends, especially the male variety."

Fenn smiled. "It seems to me that Dilly could probably take care of herself with any variety."

Isadora returned his smile. "You may be right, but I need to tell you a couple of things. Though I've tried to keep a low profile, there are those in Bostonville and elsewhere who know that I am fairly wealthy. Young fortune hunters are a problem—and there is always the fear of kidnapping."

"Kidnapping?"

"When Dilly was living in her small apartment in Medford City, an enterprising young drone, who knew Dilly would be away from her phone for a couple of days, called me. He asked for $500,000 to return her safely. Before we delivered the money, we discovered that it was a fake kidnapping. Nevertheless, it scared me."

"Wow. I never thought of kidnapping."

~~~~~~~~~~~

Fenn, now alone in the library, picked up the contract. It was difficult to internalize that Isadora Penbroke had chosen *him* for the strange enterprise of guarding her niece. Though his tall lanky body was moderately strong, it would have never entered his head that he was fit enough to be a bodyguard. He had begun weight lifting for only one reason—beefing up his muscles so he might be more attractive to the opposite sex.

One day, the owner of the training center offered him a job as personnel manager. He accepted because of the pay and because working with people gave him material for his columns.

He'd only worked at the fitness center a short time when he noticed an interesting occurrence. At one time or another, all the trainers would go out of their way to butter up Isadora Penbroke when she came in twice weekly for her light work out. Paying no attention to the furor or to Mrs. Penbroke, for that matter, he just did his job.

A month ago, however, he noticed Mrs. Penbroke watching him. Finally becoming curious, he asked the owner of the fitness center why all the trainers paid so much attention to the lady. He explained that he kept losing trainers when Mrs. Penbroke offered them a lucrative salary to be a bodyguard to her niece. Fenn laughed, finding it all quite amusing and very odd.

The surprise came two weeks ago when she approached him to be her personal trainer. He told her he wasn't trained for that, explaining that even if he were, it would interfere with the job he was hired to do.

Fenn thought that was the end of it. To his surprise the owner called him into his office, and assured him that he was qualified enough to help the wealthy dowager—as well as do his job.

As Isadora's personal trainer, he found her to be an interesting and colorful person. He liked her, but she asked too many questions. Now he could understand why.

The other trainers teased him, predicting that he would be the next bodyguard. He laughed, knowing the joke was on them. No way would Mrs. Penbroke consider his physique bodyguard material. So he thought.

Now here he was, sitting in the Penbroke library, trying to read a contract and go over an application that only brought more questions to his mind.

Isadora walked into the library. "Well?" she asked.

"I don't know how I can turn this opportunity down. But I see by some of questions in the application that you may not accept me."

"That's right."

"Could I take the contract and application form home, study them, write down some questions, and think about it for a couple of days?"

"You may take them home and study them overnight only. It would be preferable if you filled out the job application before returning it the first thing in the morning. If we can come to a mutual agreement tomorrow, I expect you to move in and be ready to go to work the next day, Wednesday."

"Wednesday? But I have to give more notice than that to the fitness center—and to my landlord."

"No, you don't. I will take care of both."

He stared at her, the full impact of what she said suddenly dawning...

"I see," he said slowly. "Money buys everything."

"Apparently, what you don't know, Mr. Dinkle," Isadora stated in crisp tones, "is that the Penbroke family owns a considerable amount of property in the city of Bostonville, making it possible to exert some influence when needed."

"Oh? I think I remember hearing a farfetched rumor about the Penbroke family, a while back."

"And—what is that?" Isadora asked in a peremptory manner.

"Somebody mentioned that the Penbroke family 'owned' Bostonville."

"Did you believe it, Fenn?"

He smiled. "Not hardly. That sounded too much like something out of a movie or a novel."

A sparkle of amusement in her eyes, Isadora said, "It happens to be true. I *own* this town."

"Well, what do you know," he smiled lazily, clasping his hands behind his head, "Now I feel like I'm *in* some kind of a movie or novel."

Isadora resisted a smile. "I expect you to be back here promptly at 8:00 in the morning. We'll cover your questions and mine, then if we can come to an agreement, I'll need to inform Dilly of it before she leaves to catch the bus."

"Whew! You are some tough lady, Isadora Penbroke," he exclaimed as he stood up, towering over her. "See you tomorrow morning at eight o'clock sharp."

Isadora walked him to the door. "Good night, Mr. Dunley Fennimore Dinkle," she said, with a stern demeanor—maintained until he turned his back—then she smiled.

# Chapter Two

Isadora opened the door at exactly 8:00 A.M. to a well groomed, clean-cut looking Fenn Dinkle. His sun-bleached blonde hair was combed to perfection. The toast-brown, cotton pants, pressed to a sharp crease, complemented the casual off-white shirt. Twinkling hazel eyes greeted Isadora, followed by a smile that spread across his face. She noticed early on that laugh lines were already beginning to form at the corners of his eyes. This, quite unusual for one so young, indicated to Isadora more than an average sense of humor, which anyone certainly needed when dealing with Dilladora. His face, also, was average until he smiled, then his whole countenance lit up, transforming him into a very nice looking young man. His long distinctive nose and slightly prominent jaw added dignity to his mien. All in all, one would look twice at Fenn Dinkle.

"Good morning, Isadora."

"Good morning, Fenn. Do come in." She led him into the library and closed the big double doors. Walking over to the two pillowed cane sofas that faced each other in front of the Italian marble fireplace, she seated herself on one, gesturing to the other. Fenn sat across from her.

Shaking his head, Fenn thumbed through the application form. "Found it downright uncomfortable answering some of these questions, Isadora."

"Oh?"

"It took some doing. I like to keep my private feelings and beliefs to myself until I know a person—and even then most people don't want to know that much. For instance, why is it important to know my political leanings and uh...when I first kissed a girl?"

"I pay the money, you answer the questions."

He threw up his hands in resignation. "Okay!" he said, then handed her the application. "You look it over and see if I pass muster. If I do, I have some more questions."

Isadora took the application and put on her glasses. Fenn fidgeted as she read through it. Several minutes later, Isadora laughed.

"You really didn't kiss a girl until you were twenty-one?"

Fenn colored slightly, but laughed good-naturedly. "And that is no one's business but mine."

Isadora, removing her glasses, frowned with concern. "Do you like girls, Fenn?"

He stared at her in surprise, then a slow grin spread across his face. "And how!"

"Then—why aren't you married?" she asked, knowing from experience with the other young men, that she was on shaky ground.

"That is what my mother keeps asking me, my father, my seven brothers and sisters, my grandparents, cousins, uncles and aunts. I get it from all directions!"

Isadora, totally taken back and amused at his disarming honesty and candidness, finally asked, "And what is the answer?"

"Doggone it, Isadora," he exclaimed as he stood up and began pacing the floor. "I'll tell you like I tell all of them—I'm trying. I keep dating, but there are so many 'ninny heads' out there, I'm frustrated as all get out. I'm not going to marry just anyone. She has to be the right one. And I'm getting darned tired of trying to find her." He sat down again, emphasizing his words with a heavy sigh.

Isadora was silent a moment, internalizing that most unusual outburst. "Thank you for being so frank, Fenn." Slipping her glasses on again, she quickly scanned the rest of the answers. She put down the application.

"Congratulations, you passed muster."

"Thanks!" he grinned. "That's the big hurdle—but I have a problem. I assume being a bodyguard you have to stand around, watch and wait. Well, I'm not good at just standing around, in fact I'm downright poor at it. You see my mind is always going and when my mind is, my hands have to be. I'm a writer, how good I don't know, but I finally got my foot in the door with a couple of papers, as I told you. I'm a human interest columnist, so I was wondering—would you object to me carrying a small note book and pen around with me so I can jot down ideas now and then?"

"That's a worthy ambition, Fenn, but Dilly will do every thing in her power to trick you, lose you, or get you in trouble so that I'll fire you. You'll have to stay on your toes. If you can jot down ideas and be totally aware, more power to you."

"Good. Now will you keep me informed of her schedule?"

"No."

"No?"

"When we both sign the contract, I wash my hands of it. You'll have to deal only with Dilly. That is, unless there is an emergency or danger involved that I need to know about."

"Doggone it, Isadora!" He stood up in frustration. "She's not going to cooperate."

"Of course not."

"When I'm up in my apartment for instance, how am I going to know when she leaves the house?"

"There is one thing that will ease your mind, Fenn. Dilly is a truthful girl and a girl of her word. If she says she will leave the house at 8:00 A.M. for the bus, she will leave then, not a minute sooner. The trick is getting her to tell you in the first place."

"I have a feeling that I'll earn every penny of your exorbitant salary."

"Shall we sign the contract, Fenn?"

He sat down and heaved a sigh, reflecting an uneasy anticipation of the future. "Yeah," he said at last, "let's sign the contract."

When they finished, Isadora glanced at her watch. Getting up, she walked out of the library and stepped across the hall to the foot of the stairs. "Dilly!"

"Yes, Aunt Issy," a voice echoed from upstairs.

"Come down a few minutes before you have to leave."

Fenn's hands felt sweaty, in fact he was sweating all over when Dilladora Dobson came running down the stairs looking glamorous and vibrant, carrying her books in a back pack which hung from her shoulder.

"Why, good morning, Dudley."

"Dunley," he corrected.

"I'm sorry...Dunley," she repeated sweetly.

"People call me Fenn, short for Fennimore."

"How nice of them, Dunley."

"Dilly!" reprimanded her aunt. "Fenn is now your new bodyguard and I would like you to cooperate with him when he requests your schedule of all activities and social engagements."

"Oh?" Her eyebrows raised, then a sly smile stole over her face. "I must be off or I'll be late for the bus...bye."

Fenn, a glazed expression on his face, watched Dilladora Dobson walk out of the library. When he heard the front door slam, he looked at Isadora.

"What have I gotten myself into?"

"More than you know," smiled Isadora, "more than you know."

# Chapter Three

Fenn, the oldest of eight children, began at an early age earning and saving for his future. By design, he owned few things, a habit of denial that began in junior high and continued through his life. Only two trips in the car, loaded with his belongings would have moved him to his new quarters, except for one thing—he had a weakness for books. He bought, devoured, collected books and always, to his consternation, they made moving a cumbersome and time-consuming job. But he worked fast and hard. By late Tuesday afternoon, he found himself totally settled, all his books placed and organized in the roomy built-in book cases. This was a far cry from the cramped efficiency apartment where his books filled the makeshift book case leaving the overflow in piles and boxes. He stood back smiling as he admired his collection, gratified that now any volume was available to him at a glance.

His fingers itched to begin working on future columns. His computer and table were placed inconspicuously at the far end of the room. However long or short the duration of his stay in this pleasant and convenient apartment, he was going to enjoy it.

Stepping to the window, he admired the beautiful grounds. Clearly, this was something to write home about, except—would they believe it? He could hardly believe it himself.

Seeing Isadora sitting on the veranda, reminded him of what was next on the agenda—reporting to her and formally introducing himself to Max and Sophie.

Running down the outside stairs, he walked quickly over to where Isadora was seated on one of the patio chairs.

"Good afternoon, Isadora."

Her face brightened. "Why, good afternoon, Fenn."

"I came to report that I'm all moved in and ready for work tomorrow morning."

She smiled. "Good. Please have a seat. Sophie is bringing out a pitcher of lemonade."

"Thank you." He sat, leaned back and stretched out his long legs. "This is a superb back yard, Isadora."

"It was Obadiah's pride and joy and Max has kept it up just as Obadiah liked it."

Sophie walked up to the table with a silver serving tray of refreshments. "Here you are, Issy Mum," she mumbled, placing the pitcher of lemonade and glasses on the table.

Fenn jumped to his feet and addressed her. "I don't believe we were formally introduced the other night. My name is Dunley Fennimore Dinkle. People call me Fenn, short for Fennimore."

Sophie, startled, looked at him. Her wary green eyes studied him a moment then she mumbled, "Nice to meet you uh...Mr. Fenn—name's Sophie."

"I'm Dilladora's new bodyguard, Sophie. But I'm sure you already know that."

Sophie cast a knowing glance at Isadora then back up at the tall, smiling young man.

"Condolences!" she said, without a hint of a smile on her face. Abruptly turning, she marched back into the kitchen.

"Thanks!" he yelled after her, then turned to Isadora. "She feels as hopeful for my success as a fish on a hook."

"That's about the size of it," stated a deep voice behind Fenn.

Fenn turned and saw Max grinning broadly. "I'm Max, Sophie's husband." He held out his big calloused hand.

"Glad to meet you, Max," Fenn said smiling, shaking his hand firmly. "My name's Fenn."

"Glad to have you aboard, Fenn, even though the waters are somewhat choppy."

"You're skeptical of my success as a bodyguard for Dilladora too, huh?" Fenn grinned.

Max laughed. "Dilly is the light of our life, but we do sit around here and hold our breath at times. Just do your best son, do your best."

"Thanks, Max. I will." He watched Max walk toward the kitchen door then he sat down. "Some vote of confidence I'm getting around here, Isadora."

"Did you expect anything else?"

"I guess not, but I'm an optimist. I think I'm going to be successful."

~~~~~~~~~~~

Dinner was outstanding, but Dilladora didn't show up. Already nervous about requesting her schedule, Fenn by now felt as edgy as a boy reading his first essay in English class. To make it worse, Isadora informed him, as she headed toward the back door to get her car, that she would be in a meeting all evening. He was on his own.

Hovering around in Isadora's magnificent library, he waited for Dilladora to arrive home. Ordinarily, the hundreds of books neatly chambered in the bookcases that climbed to the ceiling would have captured his total attention for the rest of the evening. And as he had seen in the movies, there was even a sliding ladder which served to retrieve those at the top! But right now, he couldn't even concentrate on looking at the titles.

Finally, Dilladora arrived. She dashed upstairs, totally unaware of Fenn's anxious presence. Soon, she was running back down the stairs and heading for the kitchen. Fenn waited a while then walked to the kitchen door and peeked in. Dilladora was seated at the kitchen table enjoying a generous plate of food that apparently Sophie had saved for her. Max and Sophie were also seated at the table, and the three were laughing and visiting.

The trick here, Fenn decided, was how to get information without infringing upon the family's privacy. He would now have to wait until she headed back upstairs. Pacing the floor in the library like a caged animal, he almost missed her. She was nearly to the top of the stairs before he could react..

"Miss Dobson!" he yelled, running to the foot of the stairs.

She stopped and looked down at him. "Why, Dunley, you're here."

"Yes, and all moved in. Could I please get your schedule for tomorrow?"

"I'll do better than that, I'll bring down my schedule for the next three days."

Fenn was shocked. This was not the Dilladora Dobson he had expected. Her sudden cooperation left him uneasy and suspicious.

In a moment she was down again, handing him a paper.

"Uh...could we go over it a minute?"

"Of course," she said with saccharin sweetness, and a smile to match.

"I appreciate this, Miss Dobson."

"Don't. I'm not giving you any special favors. I do this for all the poor hopefuls in the beginning."

"I see—to disarm them I presume."

She bristled. "Presume what you like."

He smiled, then studied the schedule.

WEDNESDAY: 8:00 A.M. Bus to Bostontown University
8:30-9:30 Advanced Psychology 302
10:00-11 Advanced Child Psychology 303
11:30-12:00 Lunch
12:30 P.M. Bus to Medford City
 3:30 Bus home
THURSDAY: 9:30 A.M. Bus to Bostontown University
10:00-12:00 Advanced Counseling Techniques 300
12:15 Lunch
1:00 P.M. Bus to Medford City
1:30-4:30 Modeling
4:45 Bus to Bostonville
FRIDAY: Same as Wednesday except: Bus home after last class. No bus to Medford City

"Why are you taking psychology classes?" he asked.

"Is that any of your business?"

"Nope, just curious."

"Is that all the questions?"

"For now, Miss Dobson."

"Oh call me Dilly, I hate formality." She turned to go upstairs. "Goodnight, Dunley."

"Goodnight, Dilly."

Back up in his apartment, Fenn felt hopeful and more relaxed. His fingers drummed over the computer, his mind racing. Acting as a bodyguard for Dilladora Dobson might prove to be fertile soil for many human interest stories. However, since there was a privacy clause in the contract, he would have to file them for now in his own private memoirs.

# Chapter Four

At 6:30 A.M., Sophie was startled to find Fenn Dinkle looking over her shoulder as she prepared breakfast.

"Would you mind, Sophie, if I take my meals in here? I feel like I'm intruding upon the family's privacy if I eat in the dining room with them."

She shrugged her shoulders. "It's all right with me, Mr. Fenn, but you can never tell where Mrs. Penbroke and Dilly will decide to eat. Many times it's right here in the kitchen."

"Oh? Maybe I can eat earlier or later then."

~~~~~~~~~~

At five minutes to eight, Dilly found Fenn waiting by the front door. "Johnny on the spot, I see. Good morning, Dunley."

"Good morning, Dilly." Not wanting her to notice how he was shaking in his boots, he flashed her a cheerful smile—more cheerful than he felt. Gone were the optimism and relaxed complacency of last night—both due, he was sure, to his excitement over the salary and the wonderful new surroundings. He had worked at many jobs in his life and knew something about each one beforehand, but did he know anything about this one? No! He didn't even know what to expect or how he was supposed to act. The least Isadora could have done was train him a little—like any competent employer!

"Here's a bus pass Aunt Issy insisted I give you," Dilly said, shoving it at him.

"Oh? Good," he said, relief written on his face. "That will be helpful." At the moment he could use any kind of help, no matter how small. They left the house and walked together to the bus stop.

Fenn was surprised to see the bus as full as it was in this affluent neighborhood. He surmised that this was probably for two reasons: the lack of parking space in downtown Bostonville and the efficient bus system. Each time the bus stopped, more people got on than got off. He stood up to make room for others and saw Dilly do the same.

A middle-aged man who was sitting, eyed Dilly up and down in a distasteful manner, then stood up. With a suggestive leer, he offered his seat to her.

"Why thank you, sir," she said, a glowing smile on her face. Immediately, she turned to a young mother holding a baby.

"This nice gentleman has just offered a seat to you," she said.

"Oh thank you," the weary young woman said to her benefactor.

The man, ignoring the young mother's thanks, glared at Dilly, who smiled at him sweetly, turned away, and in what could have been seen as an accident, shoved her elbow into his stomach. He grunted, his face turning scarlet with anger. Purposefully unmindful of his reaction, Dilly chatted with the mother and baby.

Fenn, watching the whole episode, swallowed hard, beginning now to understand Isadora's concern over her niece's safety.

When the bus arrived at the University, Fenn found himself pushed to the rear, while Dilly, a seasoned bus commuter, stood poised at the exit. By the time he wormed his way through the crowd and got off, she was halfway up the block.

He caught up and breathlessly asked, "Can I carry your back pack for you, Dilly?"

"Don't play Sir Galahad, Dunley. You're the hired help, remember? And—I prefer that you stay a distance behind me."

"Sorry. I have a lot to learn about being a bodyguard." He smiled, trying to act casual, allowing her to walk ahead.

The University was beautiful and had the air of the old illustrious Boston school which, Fenn had heard, it was patterned after. Tall, full-limbed trees dotted the campus, while flowers and colorful bushes enhanced the old vine-covered buildings. Seasoned, well-kept wooden benches, placed here and there on the green lawn, were already filled with students, visiting or studying.

Intrigued with the campus, he almost missed Dilly as she swerved suddenly to enter a building. He set off at a gallop. Inside, he spotted her at the top of some stairs, but by the time he got there, she had disappeared. Poking his head in each classroom, he was unable to locate her. Finally, the last room at the end of the hall revealed his charge.

Stepping inside, he ambled to the back and sat in the only remaining seat available, next to a girl. The professor, already beginning his lecture, stopped.

"May I help you, young man?"

"No, I'll just be sitting in."

"Do you have an approval slip?"

"No I uh..."

Dilly stood up. "Dr. Bonham, this is Dunley Fennimore Dinkle, my new bodyguard." She said it as if it were perfectly natural to have one. The class was dead silent.

The girl next to Fenn repeated his name loudly. "Dunley Fennimore Dinkle? Is that a real name?" The class erupted with laughter.

"Quiet!" Dr. Bonham ordered, then continued lecturing as though what had just happened was not unusual—more like a daily occurrence.

Fenn, relieved that the uproar passed quickly, settled back. However, the young woman who created it now caused Fenn greater discomfort. She was shapely, attractive and 'bare naked'—a term his family always used—her skirt, so tight and short, it was hardly there. To make it worse, the girl stole glances at him, squirmed, and crossed her legs, causing the skirt to ride up. He quickly looked straight ahead, ignoring her as best he could.

Finally, she leaned over and whispered in his ear, "You're cuter than Miss Prissy's last bodyguard."

Fenn flushed. He leaned over and whispered, still looking straight ahead, "You are the one who will need a bodyguard, Miss, if you don't cover up those thighs of yours."

Her mouth dropped open in shock, then smoldering at the rebuff, her hand shot up, jerking back and forth. "Excuse me, Dr. Bonham," she blurted out, interrupting his lecture, "Dilladora Dobson's bodyguard just threatened me!"

As if on cue, forty silent heads swivelled in Fenn's direction. Fenn, his face turning a deeper shade of red, could hardly believe the gall of this young woman. More concerned over Dilly's reaction than the professor and the class, he noticed she had turned around and was staring at him, a shocked expression on her face.

"What did he say, Miss Justin?" Dr. Bonham asked in a tired voice.

"He said I was the one who would need a bodyguard if I didn't cover up my thighs."

The boys in the class hooted and hollered. The girls glared at them and at Fenn—all the girls but one—Dilly. She was giggling.

"Quiet!" ordered the frustrated professor again. "I think, Miss Justin, you just received some good advice. It would serve you well to take it."

The boys again burst into a roar of laughter; this time the professor waited until the class settled down. Then using the episode as a springboard for a lesson in the psychology of 'mystery,' he asked questions of both the boys and the girls. The conclusion, mainly from the male section, was that a girl dressed modestly created mystery and thus was much more intriguing to the opposite sex; all this to the obvious discomfort of Miss Justin. Dilly, silent throughout, was smiling.

Dr. Bonham, ending the discussion, resumed his original lecture and the class tried to regain its focus—all except for Miss Justin and the girl next to her, who were deep in whispered conversation.

Fenn was suddenly aware of a large black spider crawling on the edge of his desk. Taking a pencil from his pocket, he smiled. Remembering what he used to do as a boy when bored with school, he coerced it onto the pencil. He amused himself by tipping the pencil up and down to keep the spider crawling on it while trying to listen to Dr. Bonham's interesting lecture. Annoyed at the whispering next door, he was about to tell them to be quiet, when he overheard Miss Justin whisper Dilly's name.

He held his breath and strained to listen. Their words weren't clear, but it was obvious they were planning to do something to Dilly!

The bell rang and the two conspirators quickly placed themselves strategically, one on each side of the door, both angling theirs heads trying to see Dilly, who was trailing behind a cluster of students.

Fenn noticed a wad of string in Miss Justin's hand and guessed what they were planning to do. For the life of him, he didn't see how they could pull it off; nevertheless, he turned in time to see Dilly approaching.

Quickly stepping over to the instigator of the plot, he asked, "Miss Justin?"

"Yes, Mr. Dinkle?" she smirked.

"I believe this is your pencil," he said, handing it to her. Miss Justin took hold of it; at the same moment she saw the crawling black spider.

"EEEEK!" she screamed, throwing the pencil to the floor. She danced around, letting out short explosive shrieks as the spider darted to and fro. Her co-conspirator followed suit.

Dilly, caught behind the group of students who stopped to watch the pandemonium, soon eased herself through and out the door, unaware of what caused it and, for that matter, totally uninterested. Fenn followed—more than eager to leave the scene of his crime, determined to keep his mouth shut in the future. At the same time he felt that he had performed admirably in his first test as a bodyguard.

Hoping the next class would be less eventful, Fenn kept an eagle eye on Dilly, determined not to lose her this time. It turned out the class was on the other side of the campus, which, since Dilly walked rapidly, they soon reached. Finding a seat as far away from females as he could get, and hiding behind a muscular young man, Fenn relaxed.

The professor, teaching the child psychology class, was an attractive woman in her thirties—probably with little practical experience of her own, Fenn mused.

"The subject today," began Mrs. Resnick, "is how working women can spot psychological problems in their children by giving them quality time rather than quantity, and I'll show you that true quality time is planned for."

The lecture began with Mrs. Resnick using examples of the well-practiced techniques she used on her own children of three, four and seven, thus in her mind, proving the proposition. At this point, Dilly began firing questions at the young professor.

"Mrs. Resnick?" asked Dilly raising her hand.

"Yes, Miss Dobson?" she answered.

"You say that true quality time is planned for?"

"Yes."

"Do you consider a mother comforting her child when he's hurt, quality time?"

"Of course."

"How can you plan for that?"

"Well, there are exceptions, of course, Miss Dobson. We all know that."

"How can a mother give quality time to that hurt child if she is at work?"

"Miss Dobson, some of us aren't as well-heeled as the Penbrokes. Some of us need to work."

"Mrs. Resnick," Dilly doggedly continued, untroubled by the professor's defensive attitude. "That is not the premise here—whether a woman has to work or not. The premise you stated was that true quality time is planned for, thereby enabling one to spot problems in children."

This spawned different reactions from the class and arguments became hot and heavy, most participants agreeing with Mrs. Resnick. Only a couple of students joined Dilly, questioning the premise.

The male students sat there like lumps, afraid of offending the vociferous female majority.

By the time the class ended, Fenn was emotionally worn out. Once on the sidewalk, he followed Dilly through a maze of students to the cafeteria where he watched her pile a tray with food—enough for three. He got two hot dogs, potato salad and a root beer, then sat three tables away. After the nourishment, such as it was, he felt better.

The bus trip to Medford City was pleasant. It first meandered through the lovely, clean, well-laid-out city of Bostonville and then through the citrus groves and vegetable farms that lay between the two. The contrast between the cities was always interesting to Fenn. Bostonville—man's dream of a California city and Medford City, the reality with its' clutter and crime, typical of what was now plaguing the sunshine state.

Thirty minutes later, the bus stopped in an undesirable area of downtown Medford City where, to Fenn's dismay, Dilly got off. He quickly followed.

Entering a building labeled Medford City Consortium Building, he watched her move to a waiting line. He, too, stood in line behind her. Not sure that this was necessary, but as a novice at this new job, he thought he ought to.

The line went faster than expected and Dilly handed the form to a man who told her to be seated, that she would be called. Intent on watching where Dilly sat, Fenn failed to realize that he was next in line.

"Yes?" The man behind the counter asked.

"Oh uh...I'm not in line."

"Could'a fooled me mister."

"Me too," Fenn grimaced, ducking out of the line, and quickly finding a seat where he could keep an eye on Dilly. Just what they were doing in this particular building Fenn had no idea. He looked around. Dilly was busy enjoying a visit with an elderly gentleman; and demonstrating a warmth and sincere interest that surprised Fenn.

He began to relax. It was obvious that he was not going to be called upon to exercise his bodyguarding duties here. Everyone seemed harmless enough. What could possibly happen?

A half hour later, a heavyset woman behind the counter yelled out, "Dobson!"

Dilly got up, walked over and stood in front of her. "I'm Dobson."

The woman studied the filled out form, then looked up frowning. "What kind of a name is Dilladora Dobson?"

Dilly smiled at her. "It's different, isn't it?"

The woman's demeanor changed, the frown gone, replaced by a friendly smile and a laugh. "Well, you should hear mine," she said, handing Dilly the form. "It's been approved."

"Thank you," Dilly said, putting it inside the back pack. Long strides took her quickly down the aisle between the counter and the long row of waiting humanity.

Fenn got up and quickly followed. He had been right. Here the day was nearly over, and except for his own unfortunate contretemps with Miss Justin, there had been only that one incident on the bus—and that may have been an anomaly. Perhaps this wouldn't be such a hard job. After all, how could any female cause a problem that a determined, resourceful man couldn't handle? As they neared the end of the row, Dilly stopped suddenly, almost causing him to bump into her. Blocking their path, Fenn saw, were long black panted legs, casually crossed. At the end of these legs were a pair of large intimidating black work boots. Both their heads turned to the owner, who was grinning through a scruffy, black two-day-old beard.

"May I please pass?" Dilly asked.

"Not unless you'll say you'll go out n' have a beer with me."

"A beer?" she asked in a sweet syrupy tone. "Oh my, no thank you, I wouldn't think of frying my brain with alcohol like yours is. Now— may I pass?"

The man's face became ugly. He reached for Dilly and just as Fenn was deciding how to handle the situation, the man was on the floor in a surprised heap. Dilly edged around him and walked quickly to the door. Fenn followed, moving sideways, as he watched the dazed man come to his senses.

Dilly stopped at the door and looked at the man on the floor who was staring at her, his mouth open—along with the rest of the row of faces.

"Ta ta," she waved and smiled, then disappeared out the door with Fenn stumbling after her.

"How...how did you do that?!" he blurted out.

Ignoring his question, Dilly walked serenely away from the building leaving a dazed Fenn to follow in her wake.

Striding down the sidewalk toward the bus stop, passing a construction site, Dilly heard whistles. Turning in their direction, she smiled and looked away. She was almost safely past when a young beefed-up construction worker, near the sidewalk, spewed out a lewd suggestion at her. She stopped. With slow deliberate steps she walked over to where he was working. Fenn couldn't see Dilly's face, but was sure her look was withering since the recipient backed up a foot or two, his eyes darting around, looking for a way to escape.

As for Fenn, he was seething. Dilly was a young woman of class! With fists clenched, he was ready and more than willing, at a moments notice, to use his status as a bodyguard! The only problem—just how much of a bodyguard *did* Dilly need?

Dilly looked over at the other workmen and called to them.

"Hey fellas, which one of you is the superintendent?"

Deciding the best course might be to act casual, Fenn leaned against a lamp post, watching and waiting.

A big-boned, gray-haired man walked over to Dilly. "I'm the superintendent, ma'am. What can I do for you?"

"My name is Miss Dobson and yours?" she asked, holding out her hand.

"My name's Roger, ma'am," he said, shaking the offered hand.

"I'm pleased to meet you, Roger. I would like to register a complaint against this man here. He made a very offensive suggestion to me as I was walking by, and I see by the wedding band on his finger that he's married." The man in question, his mouth open, stared warily at her as she fished around in her book pack. Pulling out a pad and pencil she continued. "I would appreciate it if you would give me his name and address so I can inform his wife—as to the nature of the suggestion."

Roger, totally surprised at the request, weighed the situation, noting the expression of fear on the worker's face.

"His name is..."

"Ah...boss!" the offender whined, "You wouldn't!"

"How many times have I told you to keep your filthy language off the job? And now you use it on a woman passing by?"

"I won't do it anymore, boss," he groveled. "I promise. Just don't give her my name and address—please!"

Roger looked over at Dilly questioningly.

Her eyes bore into the offender, making him almost jig with uneasiness, then she turned to Roger.

"I'll let it go this time, Roger." Turning back to the worker, her eyes boring into him again, she said, "But I would strongly suggest, mister, that you clean up your mind as well as your mouth. Your wife will be much happier. Good day, gentlemen." She turned and walked briskly toward the bus stop, leaving the two men staring after her.

Fenn had to admit, a bit begrudgingly, that Dilly handled it much better than he would have. Feeling grateful he hadn't given in to his first impulse to bloody the guy's nose, he joined Dilly at the bus stop—careful to remain, a few feet away.

The bus ride home, echoing the rest of the day, was nerve-racking. Fenn's seat was close enough to Dilly to see a young man sit beside her and hear his smooth attempt to get a date. Listening to her responses, Fenn was concerned. Surely, she wouldn't be so foolish as to go out with a perfect stranger! But then, maybe she would.

At Dilly's signal, the pair lowered their voices so he couldn't hear. Irritated, he got up and stood directly in front of them, listening while holding on to the overhead bar. Dilly glared a back-off warning at him, but he blatantly continued staring and listening.

"This man," Dilly said to her companion and pointing to Fenn, "is rude. He's trying to listen to our conversation."

The young man was startled. He looked up, then snarled, "Hey buddy, bug off!"

"No, you bug off," suggested Fenn amiably. "You happen to be sitting by my girl."

"What?" He turned to Dilly. "Is this true?"

"Of course not."

"We haven't been getting along very well today," Fenn said, shrugging his shoulders.

"You know this guy?" he asked Dilly.

"Yes but..."

"Never mind, I don't want to get into the middle of this. You can sit by your girl, mister," the young man conceded.

"Thanks, buddy, I appreciate it." Fenn smiled as he sat next to Dilly.

"How dare you?!" she hissed.

"I'm getting paid four thousand plus a month to be daring," he whispered, smiling.

"You just wait, Fenn Dinkle, you won't be around long enough to get a third of that salary!"

She turned away from him as far as she could and stared out the window. Fenn felt greatly relieved. Now he could let down his guard, at least for the duration of the bus trip home.

He had time to contemplate the events of the day. As he did so, he seriously questioned the efficacy of his decision to guard this girl—this young woman who could slay her own dragons. He felt almost useless. Oh, he did rescue Dilly from the spiteful duo, but—would Miss Justin and cohort have concocted the idea of tripping Dilly if he hadn't spouted off? Probably not. No, he was about as useless today as excess nose hair! And he had given up his apartment and job, both of which were darn hard to find in Bostonville.

When they arrived at their bus stop, Fenn was still in a lather. Getting off the bus, they separated, Dilly heading for her aunt's brownstone and Fenn around the corner to the alley driveway that led to his quarters.

Inside the apartment, he sat in one of the big comfortable chairs, leaned his head back, totally exhausted and relieved to finally be out of Dilladora Dobson's presence.

Could this day be real? Fenn asked himself. How much of what happened was Dilladora's usual approach to life, and how much was her MO for getting rid of an unwanted bodyguard? Either way, the thought of finding out left him feeling distinctly uneasy.

# Chapter Five

Something far-off was jingling and it wouldn't go away. As Fenn came to, he realized it was the telephone. He had gone to sleep in the chair! He reached out for the phone which was on the nearby lamp table.

"Hello?"

"Fenn, this is Isadora. Dinner is ready. We're eating on the veranda tonight."

"Thanks, Isadora, I'll eat later. I don't feel right about intruding upon your privacy as a family."

"You are to eat all your meals *with* the family."

"Why?"

"Dilly has been an only child. I've always imported friends to be with her."

"I'm not a friend. As Dilly put it today, I'm just the hired help." He realized that a note of irritation had crept into his voice.

"Mr. Dinkle, yours is to do, not to question."

"Yes ma'am, I'll be right down." The thought of Sophie's cooking quickly dissipated his minor irritation. He realized he was starved.

"Good evening, Isadora," he said, smiling as he walked across the veranda to the table where she was sitting. "You look mighty glamorous tonight, as usual."

"Glamorous? I've been accused of many things, but not that."

"Well-l," he drawled, sitting at the table, "Maybe I don't know what glamorous is, but it seems to me when a woman can put together unusual clothes, unusual colors and have them turn out to be classy as well as charming, in my book, that's glamour."

Isadorah smiled. "Thank you, Fenn. Obadiah liked the way I dressed."

"What about Uncle Obi?" Dilly asked, walking up to the table, and seating herself.

"Your uncle appreciated my taste in clothes."

Fenn saw for the first time a wide sincere smile on Dilly's face, and as he suspected, it was beautiful.

"He did. He appreciated everything about Aunt Issy," she said, addressing Fenn. "He was the last of the truly gallant men."

"The last?"

"Yes, I've never met a man, single or married, that measures up to Uncle Obi."

"I suspect that one of these days, someone will come along who will seem as gallant to you as your Uncle Obadiah."

"Oh, and what makes you suspect that, Mr. Bachelor? Apparently no girl has come along who is gallant enough in your eyes."

"You're right." He grinned. "Gallantry is not exactly what I'm looking for in a woman."

Sophie wheeled out a cart of wonderful looking food and the three enjoyed it in a companionable silence for some time before Isadora spoke.

"And how did your first day of work go, Fenn?"

"Dilly doesn't need a bodyguard," he said, concentrating on the food before him. "She can take care of herself."

Dilly laughed.

Isadora frowned. "Did I ask your opinion about that, Mr. Dinkle?"

"No ma'am."

"You need to fire Dunley," Dilly blurted out.

Isadora and Fenn both looked up from their plates in surprise.

"Why?" Isadora asked.

"Because he threatened a poor innocent girl in Dr. Bonham's class today, causing quite a disturbance."

Isadora, used to taking Dilly's outrageous remarks with casual disregard, found herself taken back.

"Is this true, Fenn?"

"Well not exactly—but sort of."

Dilly doubled over with laughter. Fenn's tan face suddenly had a pink cast to it. Isadora watched both, a bemused expression on her face.

"Since Dilly can't seem to get control of herself, can you tell me how and why you threatened that poor innocent girl?"

Dilly, holding in her amusement with a tight smile, focused on Fenn— waiting for the answer.

"She wasn't poor and she wasn't innocent."

This sent Dilly into gales of laughter. Fenn, not finding it amusing, glared at her. Isadora smiled.

When Dilly calmed down, Isadora again asked Fenn for details.

"I would rather not, Isadora, if you don't mind."

Dilly's laughter began all over again, further annoying Fenn.

When it finally subsided, Isadora said, "I'm waiting, Fenn."

"Well uh," he began, feeling thoroughly uncomfortable, "the only seat left was beside this uh...naked girl."

"Naked?!" exclaimed Isadora.

"Naked?" questioned Dilly, her eyes wide.

"In my book, she was. She had on a skirt so short and tight, that—I was uncomfortable. Every time she moved, crossed or uncrossed her legs, it seemed to get shorter."

"Don't tell me you were ogling, Dunley?" Dilly asked, thoroughly enjoying his discomfort.

"No ma'am. I was looking straight ahead, ignoring her the best I could."

"What happened?" Isadora asked, figuratively on the edge of her seat.

"She whispered something to me."

"And what was that?" prompted Dilly, smiling smugly.

"Say it," stated Isadora, a tinge of command in her voice.

"You are one persistent woman, Isadora."

Dilly incensed, jumped to her feet. "Isadora? You call my aunt—Isadora? You are the hired help, Dunley, remember?"

"How can I help but remember? This is the second time you've reminded me."

She looked at her aunt, waiting. With nothing forthcoming, she asked, "Aunt Issy, are you going to let him get away with calling you by your first name?"

"Calm down, Dilly. I asked him to call me Isadora."

"But...but," she spluttered, "you didn't allow any of the other body-guards to be that familiar. Why...why *him*?"

Fenn was surprised to hear about his special privilege. He grinned, "Yes, Isadora, why me?"

"Oh—I don't know." She smiled at him. "Maybe it's your casual manner and way of speaking."

"But Aunt Issy..."

"Dilly, you're making a big to-do about nothing. It's really not important, is it? If I remember right, you dislike formality with a passion. Now, Fenn, go on and tell me."

He wrestled with himself a moment, then made the decision. "Whew! What I won't do for money. Uh...the poor innocent girl said that I was uh...cuter than Dilladora's last bodyguard."

"Is that all?" asked Dilly.

"It was the straw that broke the camel's back."

"Go on," encouraged Isadora.

"I told her that she was the one who was going to need a bodyguard if she didn't cover up those thighs of hers. And then of all stupid things, the girl raised her hand and told the professor and the whole class that I had threatened her—and even told them exactly what I said."

Isadora, dumbfounded, started to laugh and Dilly joined her.

Allowing himself to see the humor, Fenn watched the two enjoy themselves at his expense, though their amusement did seem to go on for an unreasonable length of time. He would think they were through laughing, then they would start again. He chuckled between bites, enjoying his meal in spite of them.

When he was sure they were really through laughing, he spoke, "So fire me."

"Yes, Aunt Issy, fire him!" came Dilly's muffled exclamation from behind the napkin with which she was wiping her nose.

"You want me to fire you, Fenn?" Isadora asked as she wiped the tears from the corners of her eyes.

"Well, yes and no."

"Why yes?"

"Because this was one of the hardest days of my life. I'm worn out."

"Worn out doing what?" Dilly asked in disgust.

"Watching you try to set the world straight by setting it on its ear."

Isadora laughed; Dilly frowned.

Sophie brought out bowls of strawberries for dessert, fresh from Max's garden.

"Thank you for the great meal, Sophie," Fenn said. "My mother would admire your cooking immensely, and she's a mighty good cook herself."

Sophie's full lips spread across her face into a big toothy smile. "That's a nice compliment, Mr. Fenn."

The three savored the sweet strawberries. When they were through, Dilly gathered the empty bowls and stood up.

"Well, Aunt Issy—are you going to fire him?"

Isadora studied her niece a moment then smiled. "Well now, Dilly—I think I'll give him a raise instead."

Fenn's jaw dropped. It was his turn to laugh, which he did heartily while watching Dilly's shock turn to indignation. With an abrupt flip of her head, she stomped into the kitchen, slamming the screen door.

Fenn, realizing he was still on the job, swallowed his laughter. Standing up he gathered the empty glasses.

"Excuse me, Isadora, I have to speak to Dilly, so I'll carry these to the kitchen." He found Dilly washing pans, a little too fast and furious, he thought. Sophie was putting food away.

"May I dry the dishes?" Fenn asked.

"We have a dish washer, Dunley."

"May I dry the pans then?"

"Polishing apples are you, Dunley?"

"No, ma'am, just pans," he said grinning. "It's a habit, I guess, helping with the dishes. I grew up having to help with the dishes every night, since there were eight of us kids."

Dilly stopped and stared at him. "Eight?"

"Yep, eight."

"I was an only child," she said to the dishwater. A wistful expression lingering in her eyes.

"I'm sorry. You did miss out."

"You *liked* being in that big a family?"

"You bet."

Dilly was silent, washing the pans more slowly now. Fenn found a dish towel and began wiping them as he formulated his next question for Dilly.

"Do you plan on staying home tonight or are you going out?" he asked cautiously.

A little smile played around Dilly's lips. "Wouldn't you like to know?"

"Yes ma'am, I would."

Dilly laughed. "I haven't decided."

"When will you decide?"

"I don't know."

"Doesn't it get tiresome?"

"What do you mean?'

"Trying to get the bodyguards fired or to quit."

"Very!" she said, throwing a large ladle into the soapy water for emphasis.

"Then why don't you quit wasting energy over it and accept it?" Fenn questioned.

"How would you like someone following you everywhere?" she snapped, renewing her attack on the offending ladle.

"I wouldn't. If I were you, I would quit doing the things that worry your aunt, then she wouldn't feel like you needed protection."

The scrubbing came to an abrupt halt. Turning slowly, her hand still grasping the dripping ladle, she took a step toward him.

Unsure of her intentions, and startled by the sudden fire in her eyes, Fenn involuntarily took a step backward.

After a long moment of silence, she tilted her head to one side. "My, my," she said, her voice dripping with sarcasm, "only one day on the job and you're already giving me advice? I'm sorry, Mr. Dunley Fennimore Dinkle, but giving advice is not part of your job."

Recovering his aplomb, he shot back, "In my book it is. And you can expect more of it, Miss Dilladora Dobson."

"In that case," she said imperiously, as she stepped to the sink dropping the ladle back in, "I won't tell you whether I'm going out tonight—or any other night for that matter."

"Wel-ll, Dillweed" he drawled, "if you're going to act like a spoiled brat, I'll just have to treat you like one." He thought he heard a snicker behind him from Sophie.

"How dare you call me Dillweed?!"

"How dare you call me Dunley when I prefer Fenn?"

"Oh!" she exploded. Her hand came out of the water clutching the dripping dishcloth. With an abrupt whip of her arm, she slammed the inoffensive cloth back into the sink, raising a geyser of soapy water, soaking herself and splashing Fenn. Putting wet hands upon her hips, she glared at him, suds dripping from her nose and chin.

"You are the biggest smart mouth Aunt Issy has hired yet!"

"Thank you," he grinned, seeming to find amusement in her outburst.

"Ooh! You know," she began, her eyes narrowing as she wiped the suds off her chin and nose with the back of her hand, "I can move out of here, back on my own as before, and you would be out of this cushy, lucrative job."

"Wel-ll, as Clark Gable said in *Gone With the Wind*, 'Frankly my dear, I don't give a darn.'"

She stared at him—then giggled. "That's not what he said."

"I know, but I don't swear."

Dilly scrutinized him, her mouth open—strange half-choking sounds were coming from her throat. She stumbled over to the table, sat, put her head down on her arms and laughed uncontrollably. Sophie, who was chuckling, looked over at Fenn, who in turn, grinned and shrugged his shoulders.

Max walked into the kitchen. Seeing Dilly, he looked over at Sophie in concern, "Is she crying?"

"No, she's laughing."

"Oh," he said, smiling with relief.

Dilly finally looked up, tears streaming down her face—nose running.

"All right, Mr. Dunley-Do-Right, I am not going out. Just get out of my sight!"

"Thank you." He grinned and tossed the dish towel to Max. "Goodnight, Max, Sophie. See you in the morning, Miss—Dilly-Do-Right."

~~~~~~~~~~~

The short nap and the subsequent meal had revived Fenn. This, coupled with the raise hinted at by Isadora, made him feel more confident in his decision to give up both job and apartment to work for her.

Why she was pleased enough to give him a raise, he wasn't quite sure, but he didn't want to analyze it too carefully.

Eager to take advantage of the free evening, he decided it was time to write home and fill the family in on the new and strange events of his life. Smiling, he thought about their reaction, especially that of his fifteen-year old brother. Andy, he knew would find it hilarious that anyone with his physique would be hired as a bodyguard and would probably write him a letter teasing him unmercifully. Fenn chuckled.

"Dear Mom, Dad and Family," the letter began.

"I now have a cook, a gardener and a full set of book cases to house all my books." He smiled, wishing he could see their faces when they read this first sentence.

Loving a good story and having a tendency to make a good story better, Fenn would sometimes embellish the facts, as his family knew only too well. But in this case, truth was stranger than fiction—such as the wealthy and glamorous Isadora Penbroke owning a town! Who would believe that in this day and age? Not his family. He chuckled again as he wrote about Isadora.

Describing Dilladora, however, was another matter. In the short time he'd known her, she'd proved to be a bundle of contradictions. After much thought, the only thing that came to mind was—he hadn't figured her out yet.

Thus, he wrote: "Isadora's niece, the beautiful and enigmatic Dilladora, heiress to the Penbroke fortune, became the target of a spurious kidnapping. Because of this and because of Dilladora's daring ways and disregard for danger, her anxious aunt hired a bodyguard to follow her everywhere. Totally incensed over this turn of events, the headstrong niece soon managed to get him fired. The determined aunt hired another one and the just-as-determined niece, knowing the stipulations in the contract signed by Isadora and the bodyguard, aided the latter in his downfall. So it went, one after the other. To date, Dilladora, a very bright and clever lass, has tripped up each hapless aspirant."

"So you see, I'm one of a long line of 'unsophisticates.' Already, after only one day, the fiery redheaded Miss Dobson has requested, for reasons totally unwarranted, that her aunt fire me. The demise of my new career as bodyguard may be imminent—but until then, I'm going to do all in my power to outwit the beautiful damsel. And while I'm at it—enjoy the adventure."

This was as accurate a description of Dilladora and the situation as he could come up with, given no embellishments—as it needed none. He knew it would have his family on the edge of their seats.

He had intended to write a column for the papers but the letter to his family took all evening. A thorough writer, he described in detail how he had been hired by Isadora Penbroke, describing her brownstone, the yard and Sophie and Max. And of course he had to relate the experiences of the first day on the job.

After printing a copy for the family and one for his memoirs, it was 10:00 P.M. Since tomorrow was the deadline for the columns, he would fax the newspapers one from several he'd written ahead.

Fenn leaned back in his chair and stretched, then picked up Dilly's schedule and studied it—wondering what was in store for him tomorrow. The thought crossed his mind that he might set a record—the record of being the first of Dilladora Dobson's bodyguards to be fired after only two days...

# Chapter Six

Fenn was greeted at breakfast by Isadora with a warmth that hadn't been there before. And Sophie's resolute demeanor softened into a smile as she placed a glass of juice in front of him. He wasn't surprised at Dilladora's coolness; the surprise came from the other two. Somehow, he was in their good graces and had no clue as to why. But accepting his good fortune, his natural optimism soared. Maybe this job would last a day or two longer after all.

The bus, less crowded than the previous day, had a space near the driver on one of the side seats. Here, Fenn could keep an eye on Dilly and get off when she did. Not acknowledging his presence in the slightest, Dilly sat on the first seat facing the front.

Taking advantage of the opportunity, he pulled out his note book and pen and began jotting down ideas for his columns. His fingers flew, ideas coming fast and clear. He glanced up and saw Dilly watching him with curiosity. She quickly looked away.

He found the class on Advanced Counseling Techniques, taught by the same Dr. Bonham, much to his liking. He was fascinated by Dr. Bonham's wisdom and understanding, and the two hours passed quickly. While taking notes, he wondered why Dilly was taking these psychology classes and why, at her age, she was still in school.

The class ended and Fenn took a few moments to finish jotting down the last of his notes. Putting his notebook and pen away, he looked for Dilly. She wasn't in the room.

Squeezing through and pushing past students, he finally made his way to the hall. Looking ahead as he wove in and out of the incoming and outgoing crowd, he still couldn't see her. Lunch was next on the schedule, so he walked toward the cafeteria, certain he'd find her there. His eyes searched the cafeteria. No Dilly. Sitting at a table where he could clearly see the entrance and exit, he watched and waited, not feeling too concerned. However, as the minutes passed with no sign of his charge, a vague uneasiness took hold. At 12:50 he realized, with a start, that Dilly had ditched him!

"Doggone that girl!" he muttered to himself as he hurried out of the cafeteria. Out on the sidewalk, he broke into a run and reached the bus stop just as the Medford City bus departed.

"Dang!" he blurted out, realizing that he didn't know when the next one would come along or if there was a next one. Asking several students failed to enlighten him.

Pacing the sidewalk, he fumed. Though cognizant from the beginning that this was going to be a contest of wills, the reality of it fired his determination. Miss 'Dillweed Dobson' was going to get the contest of her life!

Debating whether to run back to the cafeteria to phone the bus company and take the chance of missing the next one, or just sit and wait, he chose the latter. His stomach growled, reminding him that he hadn't eaten lunch.

Two-and-a-half hours later, the Medford City bus arrived. Feeling a slight panic as he got on, he had to remind himself of Isadora's statement that Dilly was a girl of her word. He calculated that it would take fifteen minutes to the Bostonville city limits and another fifteen minutes to Medford City and maybe another ten or fifteen minutes to where Dilly was modeling. Then it hit him. He didn't know where she was modeling! She had omitted that piece of information. He couldn't believe how careless and naive he'd been. Contemplating his plight, he was baffled. Fifteen minutes later, still in a sweat, he took a seat up near the bus driver.

"Excuse me, sir, do you know of a place in Medford City where uh...I mean could you tell me where I might get off close to a modeling agency?"

"There are three. Which one do you want to go to?"

"I don't know," he said, miserably. "I don't know the name of it."

"I wish I could help you, but..."

"I don't suppose you remember, by any chance, uh...a beautiful redhead getting off near one?"

"Oh, I know one all right, but I doubt if she's the one."

"Her name is—you probably wouldn't know her name, you see so many passengers—thanks anyway."

"I know this girl's name."

"Oh?"

"It's Dilladora Dobson."

"That's the one!" Fenn almost shouted.

"She gets off across the street from the Fashion Fare building where she models. I'll tell you when."

"Thank you. I appreciate this more than you know." He grinned, hardly able to believe his good fortune. He noticed that this driver was not the same as yesterday.

"You a friend of Dilladora's?" the driver asked.

"No, I'm her bodyguard."

"Great guns! She didn't have one Tuesday. You're the new one?"

"Yes sir," Fenn replied in surprise.

"Am I glad to meet *you*. My name is Joe and yours?"

"Fenn."

"This is a bit of luck, Fenn, having you here without Dilladora."

"Oh?"

"Would you do me a big favor?"

"Be glad to, Joe."

"Would you mind not letting Dilladora run alongside the bus?"

"Run alongside the bus! What do you mean?"

"She's always late. I..." He looked around then lowered his voice. "I hold the bus as long as I can, but invariably, just as I start up, she comes running alongside the bus 'till she reaches the doors, then waves at me until I open them. It's downright dangerous."

"Don't wait for her," suggested Fenn, totally at a loss why this was a problem.

"Well," began Joe, a little sheepishly, "I'm afraid I'm a little soft when it comes to Dilladora—I only wait five minutes," he quickly assured him.

Fenn was amused. "I'll do the best I can to keep her from running alongside of the bus but she's studied some kind of martial arts. I saw her topple a big guy onto the floor before he knew what was happening.

Joe laughed. "She's taken jujitsu."

"Hey, I've taken a little of that. Thanks for the information. I may be able to block her moves if she tries it on me—but then it's more likely that I won't." They both laughed.

"I couldn't get any one of the past bodyguards to stop Dilladora from running after the bus. They each told me it was against the contract to even touch her."

"It is. But the way it's going, Joe, I'll probably get fired in a couple of days anyway, so no way am I going to allow her to be foolhardy. I hope."

Joe smiled. "She's pretty athletic. Claims jokingly that she was a track star. It may be true."

They arrived in Medford City and Fenn saw that it was 4:00 P.M. "How long before my stop, Joe?"

"About ten minutes."

"What is the correct time that this bus is supposed to leave?"

"Four-forty," he whispered. "But I hold it 'till 4:45 for Dilladora."

Some minutes later they arrived at the Fashion Fare stop. Fenn looked at his watch.

"It's now 4:20 Joe. We'll see you at 4:40 or not at all," he said with more conviction than he felt.

# Chapter Seven

Though the Fashion Fare building was large with several entrances, Fenn finally found a street entrance on the far right marked Bernard Dumas Fashion Photographer. He figured he had the right place. Stepping inside, he entered a short hallway which led him to a good sized room cluttered with sets and cameras.

The first thing that caught his eye was a makeshift dressing cubicle out of which clothes came flying, one by one.

"Catch these, Mavis," yelled a voice from behind the screen. "I'm almost late for the bus."

The woman called Mavis, scrambled to catch them.

"We have one more shoot, Dilly, you can't leave yet!" shouted a man, who Fenn identified as the probable proprietor. This last was shouted as he slid new film into the camera.

"Bernie, how many times have I told you that I will only work three hours?"

"Dammit, Dilly, I could put you on the front pages of national magazines if you'd give me just a few more hours a week."

"You've said that before, Bernie," a muffled voice pointed out.

"You don't believe me."

"Yes I do."

"Then why have you never answered me? Why aren't you interested in becoming a nationally famous model?"

No answer came from behind the screen.

"How about internationally famous then?"

Still no answer.

"You don't need the money," he challenged.

"I need the money, Bernie," Dilly said, appearing in an attractive rumpled state. Kissing him on the cheek, she smiled. "I just don't need the notoriety. It would bore me silly. I'll see you day after tomorrow—'bye Bernie, 'bye Mavis." She ran to the door and bumped into Fenn.

"Dunley!" she gasped—shocked.

"Dillweed," he returned, grinning.

Her eyes flashed with anger. "Don't call me that!"

"Don't call me Dunley."

"Let me by, you'll make me late for the bus."

"You made me two-and-a-half hours late for the bus."

"That's your problem."

"I'm sorry, Miss Dobson," he said still blocking the doorway, "but you've already missed the bus, it is 4:41."

"No I haven't." She ducked under his arm and ran.

Fenn ran after her, but she was out the front door, sprinting for the bus even faster than he'd anticipated.

"All right, Dillweed, I was a track star too," he muttered under his breath.

She had crossed the street, and was just about to make her usual dash for the door of the slowly moving bus, when he caught up and grabbed her around the waist from behind.

Startled, Dilly shrieked. Her head jerking back toward her captor— she shrieked again, "Dunley! How dare you? Let me go!"

"No," he grunted, still holding her in a tight vice. As her squirming became more violent, the strap of the back pack loosened, slipping off her shoulder. It landed with a thud on top of his little toe.

"Ow!" he yelped, struggling to retain his hold on her.

Dilly, unaware of his yelp of pain, was stunned to see the bus pick up speed, heading on its way to Bostonville. Fenn also watched the bus, amazed that he'd managed to stop her.

"Let go of me," she demanded, thoroughly amazed at his strength. "Let go, you...you ungainly Tarzan!"

"Gladly," he groaned, dropping his arms, certain that his toe was broken.

She turned and faced him, fire blazing in her blue eyes. "Do you realize that this is the last bus to Bostonville 'till 10:00 P.M.?"

"Really?" he responded, gasping for breath.

"And what do you propose we do now?"

"What do *you* propose?"

"It's your responsibility, Mr. Dunley Dinkle. You caused us to miss the bus."

"No, I didn't, you were three minutes late by the time you reached the bus stop and it was already moving."

"That doesn't matter, I always get on."

"Dang it, Dilladora, it's dangerous to run alongside a moving bus!"

She squinted, her eyes suddenly filled with suspicion. "How did you know I do that?"

"It's my job to know these things."

"You've been talking to Joe!"

"Yeah," he said, grinning. "And I found him to be a darn nice guy. He's concerned about you and I owe him one for letting me in on your bad habit. And—while I'm around, Miss Dilly Dobson, you are not going to do it."

A slow smile spread across her face. "While you're around? Well, Mr. Dinkle, I don't think you'll be around very long when I inform Aunt Issy how you attacked me this afternoon."

"Attacked?" Fenn laughed.

"It says in the contract that you are not to touch me."

"I know." He thought about this a moment. "What is the longest time a bodyguard was able to stay on the job?"

"Two months."

"What is the shortest time?"

"Six weeks."

"What a bunch of astute fellows. I suspect then that I'll set the record for being the first of your bodyguards to be fired in—two days."

Dilly giggled. The giggles escalated into laughter. She sat on the bus stop bench and doubled over.

Fenn chuckled. In all his life, he'd never seen a girl who saw such humor in little things—not even his sisters could match her.

Finally, her head still down, the laughter slowly subsiding, Dilly held out her hand.

"Do you have a tissue? My nose is running."

"I do." He handed her a clean neatly folded white handkerchief.

Dilly took it. As she started to raise it to her nose, she stopped and scrutinized it. "You use handkerchiefs?" she asked incredulously.

"You bet. What's good enough for my father, is just fine with me. Besides," he added, "tissues make me sneeze."

"I can't blow my nose on your handkerchief!"

"Why not, I do."

Hesitating a moment, she mumbled, "Thanks," and blew her nose with complete unladylike abandon. "You are a first-rate irritation," she stated in muffled tones as she wiped her nose. "This is twice you've made my nose run."

Fenn laughed. "Thoroughly unintentional but glad to oblige." He sat on the bench beside her to rest his throbbing toe. A balmy, late afternoon breeze rustled a palm tree near by. He heaved a sigh. This was a pleasant change from his hectic day.

"You've managed to wear me out again today, Dilly. It's good to rest a minute."

Apparently, Dilly found it restful also, Fenn thought, for she sat there silent.

Dilly contemplated her unusual circumstance. This man had just physically disrupted her routine. He'd come into her life like all the other nine bodyguards had—but he was different. He dared touch her—he dared to challenge her every time she opened her mouth. She glanced over at him and saw his eyes gazing into the clouds so she studied him out of the corner of her eye. He was built differently from the others. His hands weren't huge and beefy like those of the other bodyguard's, but they were strong looking, tan and masculine. Realizing her heart was beating a little faster, she quickly chastised herself. This man has no ambition! Here he is—thirty years old, only a weight trainer, and now her bodyguard—unless...

Fenn reluctantly spoke, "You need to call your aunt and tell her that we've missed the bus. How late will the Fashion Fare building be open? I suppose you can call from there."

"They're open until 8:00, I'll call from there," she agreed, making no move to get up.

"So you don't want to have your face on the cover of a magazine and become a nationally and internationally famous model?"

"You heard all that?"

"Sure did. And, I might add, I admire you for it."

"Don't butter me up, Dunley, it won't do any good."

"Do you have any money in your back pack?"

"What?"

"Do you have any money to pay for the taxi? I'm not paying for it."

Her mouth dropped open. "You certainly are not a gentleman."

He grinned. "Nope, I'm just the hired help."

Dilly, suddenly motivated, got up and walked off in a huff toward the Fashion Fare building. Her faithful, but limping, bodyguard followed, doing his best to keep up.

While they waited in the building for the taxi, Dilly sat just inside the studio door—while Fenn, determined not to lose sight of her, also sat just inside, but on the opposite side of the opening. Bright flood lights were directed toward the set, leaving the rest of the room dimly lit except in one corner where a pair of screens created a makeshift dressing room.

Fenn watched with fascination as Bernard Dumas took pictures of beautiful girls putting on alluring and provocative expressions while posing in elegant clothes.

Dilly, bored with it all, studied one of her psychology books in the dim light.

Four chattering, giggling girls came rushing in through the doorway, not noticing Fenn or Dilly. Three of them headed toward the small dressing area, the fourth dashed to the small cubicle Dilly had used earlier.

Soon a petulant looking blonde came flouncing out of the corner dressing area. "Bernie, Millie is using the cubicle."

"So?"

"I want to use it; there isn't enough privacy in the corner."

"Since when did that bother you, Babs?"

"Since now," she pouted. "How come you built a private place for Dilladora Dobson?"

"Because she asked for it and wouldn't work if I didn't."

"Well, I won't work if you don't build me one."

"When you get serious about being modest, I will Babs," he said, his eyes pointing to her low-cut top then to the skimpy skirt.

"Humph!" Tossing her head, Babs walked back to the corner, while Fenn gawked at the exaggerated movement of her shapely hips. His eyes moved to the other girls in the dressing area who were not making use of the screen, but were openly disrobing to their underwear. Embarrassed, he jumped up and ducked out into the hall.

Dilly giggled. Soon she saw his arm reach in backwards and pull the chair out through the door to the hall. He sat in the hallway, no longer fascinated with the modeling business.

Still giggling, Dilly asked, "What are you doing out there, Dunley?"

"Waiting to trip the taxi driver, Dillweed."

"Don't call me that here!" she whispered vehemently. "If any of the girls hear that, they'll have a heyday with it."

"Don't call me Dunley," he whispered back, "they'll have a heyday with *that*."

"But I have to work here."

"So do I," he whispered. "In fact, I'm working right now."

Ooh! she thought to herself. Not for long.

~~~~~~~~~~~

The taxi ride to Bostonville was a silent one. Fenn leaned back his head and fell asleep. He awakened just as they arrived, and just as Dilly was telling the taxi driver, "The gentleman here will be paying the fare."

Pretending to just awaken, he quickly got out of the cab, and trying his best not to limp, started off down the sidewalk as quickly as he could.

Turning back, he yelled, "See you later Dilly." He resumed his quickened pace to the corner, pleased with himself for beating Dilly at her own game. As he turned the corner out of sight, he slowed and grimaced from the pain of his throbbing toe. He hobbled to his apartment.

Relieved, once again, to be out of Dilladora's presence, he freshened up and sat down to relieve his toe of the constricting shoe. However, before he could do so, his stomach growled, reminding him that he hadn't eaten since breakfast.

Immediately, he got up and limped down the stairs, across the veranda and into the kitchen. He saw no one about but was glad to see pots still on the stove and three places set at the table. Though it was 7:30, apparently Isadora had waited for them. Spying a bowl of freshly washed grapes on the counter, he grabbed a bunch and began devouring the succulent fruit just as Sophie walked in.

"Good evening, Mr. Fenn," she said, obviously glad to see him. "Good evening, Sophie. I hope you don't mind me eating some grapes, I haven't had lunch."

"How come, Mr. Fenn?" she asked with concern.

"It's a long story, Sophie."

"Hmph! Dilladora's been up to her ways again sounds like."

Fenn laughed. "Yes, she's been up to her ways." He limped over to the table carrying the bowl of grapes.

Dilly walked in and glared at him. "You hogging the grapes, Dunley?"

He smiled. "That I am, Dillweed. I didn't get lunch today. It might have something to do with the time I spent watching and waiting at the cafeteria, then sitting two-and-a-half hours at the bus stop."

"Poor Dunley," Dilly commiserated.

"Yes, poor Dunley," remarked Isadora who heard the exchange as she came in. "And why didn't poor Dunley get any lunch, Dilly?"

"Because he's not very astute, Aunt Issy. I ditched him." A triumphant smile spread over her face.

Isadora gave her niece a disapproving look, then smiled at Fenn. "Let's dine, shall we? I'm starving too."

Fenn was so hungry he almost ate more than Dilly—but not quite.

Fenn was grateful that the meal had progressed enough to satisfy some of his hunger before Isadora asked her first question.

"How did the day go, aside from missing your lunch, Fenn?"

He and Dilly exchanged glances. "Well-l," he drawled, "I surely did enjoy Dr. Bonham's class. I even took notes."

"Ha!" exclaimed Dilly. "How can a man who makes a living being a weight trainer and a bodyguard understand psychology?"

"Maybe you could explain it to me sometime."

"Fat chance."

"How was your day, Dilly?" asked her aunt.

Isadora noticed another exchange of glances between Fenn and Dilly.

"I uh...had a good day—except for missing the bus."

Fenn waited for her to go on and tell Isadora how he had 'attacked' her, but she was silent. He smiled, remembering her threats today—

empty threats as it turned out. He realized Dilly didn't want Isadora to know about her dangerous little habit of chasing the bus.

At least, he still had a job. For now anyway.

# Chapter Eight

Fenn stepped out of bed at 6:00 A.M. and groaned in pain. Looking down at the small appendage, he saw that is was swollen and blue. He groaned again. "How in the heck am I going to get my shoe on?"

Determined to ignore the pain, he got up, showered, pressed his shirt and pants, sat down and carefully put on his socks, then shoved his foot into a shoe. "Yikes!" he yelped.

He hobbled down the stairs and made it to the kitchen at 7:00 only to see no breakfast being served there.

"Good morning, Sophie."

"Mr. Fenn, breakfast is in the dining room this morning."

"Thanks, Sophie." He started toward the door when Sophie noticed his limp for the first time. "Mr. Fenn, what's the matter? You're limping!"

"Just hurt my toe, Sophie."

"You sit right down here in the kitchen," she ordered. "I'll bring breakfast to you."

"I'd be much obliged, Sophie," he said with relief.

Sophie marched into the dining room where Dilly and Isadora were filling their plates, and promptly announced, "Mr. Fenn has been wounded!"

"What?" Isadora and Dilly asked simultaneously.

"He's in the kitchen."

They both quickly followed Sophie.

Fenn looked up, surprised to see all three, trailing one after the other. He grinned. "What's this, the marching brigade?"

"Where are you hurt?" Isadora asked.

"Hurt?"

"Yes hurt," reiterated Dilly. "Sophie said you were wounded, but—you don't look wounded to me."

"Wounded?"

"Quit repeating everything we say," Dilly demanded.

Fenn laughed. "Yes, I'm wounded—it's a battle wound."

"Were you wounded in a war?" Isadora asked very concerned now.

Fenn laughed again. "Yes, I was wounded in a war, but it only happened yesterday."

"Yesterday?" questioned Isadora, puzzled.

"How?" Dilly questioned, doubt and suspicion in her voice.

"Your back pack fell on my toe."

Her eyes, narrow with skepticism suddenly opened wide, the light dawning. "Oh—my book pack is very heavy."

"I know."

"Take off your shoe and let me look at it," she ordered.

"Why?"

"Do as I say, Dunley I want to see this...this alleged wound of yours."

"Yes ma'am."

He untied his shoe and pulled his foot out, wincing as he did so. Dilly took over and gently began pulling off his sock.

"Well, if you aren't a bundle of contradictions, Dilladora Dobson."

"Why?"

"I didn't know you could be so gentle."

"I used to work as a nurse's aide in high school. Oh!" she gasped. "This looks terrible. How did you ever get this shoe on?"

"I just shoved it in."

"Ouch!" she muttered. "You shouldn't have done that. Sophie, we need an ice pack and an elastic bandage. It may be broken. You can't wear a shoe on this foot, Dunley. Do you have some loose house slippers?"

"Yes, some very loose ones. They are so old, they're about to fall apart."

"Good, I'll go get them. Is your door locked?"

"No. They're in the closet in the bedroom. Thanks!"

Dilly dashed out the door. Isadora had been sitting at the kitchen table watching the whole episode with great interest.

"I'm sorry about this, Fenn," she said.

"Don't worry about it, Isadora, it will heal quickly, but I *am* concerned about being able to keep up with Dilly now. She's the fastest girl I've ever seen."

Isadora smiled. "She was a track star in high school."

"That figures, but lucky for me, I was too."

"What really happened yesterday, Fenn?"

"Don't worry, Isadora, so far I've been able to keep her safe. I would tell you if it were otherwise."

"Good," she said.

Dilly opened the door to Fenn's apartment and was stunned. It was the first time she had seen books in that bookcase, let alone crammed full. Walking over to it, she glanced at some of the titles. There were many old history books, books on journalism, biographies of America's founding fathers, books on finance, computers and others.

She looked around the room and saw a computer, a printer, a fax machine—and wondered.

Finding the bedroom as neat as the front room with its nicely made bed, she muttered, "What a neat-freak!" The only thing left out was the ironing board and iron and she was sure it too would be put away now that it was cool. I ought to take him up to my room and give him a good scare, she thought, a small mischievous smile on her face.

She decided to nose around further. In the bathroom, everything was in its place, the towels neatly folded.

"Ugh! His poor wife someday. He'll drive her up the wall", she said, judging his future wife by herself.

Bored with being nosey, she went to the closet and found the slippers neatly placed together. She chuckled. "The poor tattered things." Picking up the left one, she saw that the sole was coming away from the side. "This will be perfect housing for his bludgeoned toe," she announced to no one in particular.

Dilly found Aunt Issy and Sophie fussing over Fenn as he ate breakfast. An ice pack, carefully placed on his wounded toe, was taking care of the pain and swelling.

Holding up the slipper for all to see, she snickered, "Perfect, huh?"

Isadora and Sophie laughed.

"Hey," Fenn complained. "I'm sentimentally attached to those slippers, folks."

Seeing that Sophie had transferred everyone's breakfast to the kitchen table, Dilly didn't waste any time disposing of her bowl of fruit and French toast.

Some minutes later, Fenn looked at his watch. "It's 7:55. We're going to be late for the bus. May I drive us?"

"Do you have a stick shift?"

"Yes."

"Then I don't suppose you can because of your toe. I'll call us a taxi."

"That's too expensive."

"Tell me about it, Mr. Dinkle." She got up and walked around the table and knelt before him. "Hand me your foot please." He did as she asked. "The swelling has stopped, for now anyway." Picking up his sock, she carefully slipped it on, then took the elastic bandage and wrapped it around lightly. "This is just to protect it in case you bump it." She noticed his nicely creased pants.

"Did you just press your pants this morning?"

"Yes," he replied, surprised.

"You mean you stood on your sore toe and pressed pants?"

"Yes—so?"

"Don't you know that rumpled is in, Dunley?"

"It is? Wel-ll," he drawled, "I don't go in much for the fads of fashion."

"Obviously."

"But," he grinned, "You on the other hand, make rumpled look mighty good."

She ignored the compliment, but smiled as she carefully placed the slipper onto his foot. "There, how does your toe feel now?"

"About a hundred percent better. What can I do to thank you?"

"Quit your job," she said, smiling sweetly as she stood up.

"Thanks," he said, grinning, "but I think I'll just wait and be fired, which you assure me won't be long."

Dilly giggled. "That's right."

"Would you do me a favor, Dilly?" he asked, his face suddenly serious.

"A favor?" she questioned, surprised. "What?"

"Don't try to ditch me today," he pleaded.

Dilly stared at him in surprise, then squelched a laugh. "Did you hear that Aunt Issy? He thinks he should get special treatment from me because his toe is hurt." Unable to hold it any longer, she burst out laughing. Finding herself unable to stop, she sat at the table and covered her face. Her laughter proved infectious to Sophie and Isadora, who found themselves joining in. Fenn, trying to remain serious, found it impossible. Soon, they were all laughing. Finally Dilly held out her hand, revealing one half of her face. Fenn could see the tears and the runny nose. He obliged her by reaching into his pocket for a hanky, and placing it into her outstretched hand. Her laughter subsided slightly, and her eyes widened as she focused on the cloth. She looked up at Fenn. "Do you press your hankies too?" she asked in amazement.

"And what if I do," he stated defensively.

"Oh no!" Laughing and choking, she could only press the hanky to her nose. When finally in control, she blew it soundly, stood up and shook her head.

"Well, Dunley, you did it again."

"Did what?"

"Made my nose run." Fenn opened his mouth to speak but she cut him off. "I'm going to go call a taxi—ready or not, I'm going to school." She got up and quickly left the kitchen.

Fenn smiled. "As I said to myself yesterday, Isadora, she is the 'laughingest' girl I've ever known."

Isadora chuckled. "She is for a fact. Her Uncle Obadiah had a sense of humor like that. Together, they could find more to laugh about than you can possibly imagine."

# Chapter Nine

As soon as the taxi arrived at the University, Dilly got out and ran, this time leaving Fenn to pay the tab. Considering his lack of mobility, he had expected just such a tactic. When he got through paying the driver, Fenn looked down the sidewalk for her. She was nowhere to be seen. Not concerned in the slightest, he confidently limped toward Dr. Bonham's class.

Edgy about running into the infamous Miss Justin while in this condition, he peered into the class room and gratefully noticed an empty seat on the front row beside Dilly.

"Saving this for me?" he asked, grinning as he sat beside her.

"Don't sit here," Dilly said, alarmed. "Go to the back."

"I'm afraid of that 'poor innocent girl.'"

Dilly stifled a giggle. "If you sit here, I warn you—don't you dare make me laugh."

"I won't utter a word. Scout's Honor," he said, thrusting three fingers into the air.

"All right, but just this once." Throughout the lecture, she was very aware of his presence. Noticing him taking notes, she sneaked a glance now and then, wondering if he had gone to college. If he had, why was he wasting his mind being a weight trainer? She was also curious about what he was writing in his little notebook on the bus. He was becoming an enigma and it both annoyed and intrigued her.

Dora May Justin sat at the back of the class, an ugly expression on her face. All she wanted was an opportunity to get back at Fenn Dinkle. When the class ended, she watched with great curiosity as he limped toward the door. Dilly followed close behind. When they were almost there, she blocked their path.

"Did you hurt yourself, Mr. Dinkle?" she asked sneeringly. "Maybe while protecting Miss Priss?" She looked down at his foot and saw the tattered house slipper. "My, my, are we poor? Isn't Dilladora's auntie paying you enough?"

Fenn ignored her, but Dora May continued, "Did Dilladora stomp on your foot—like this?"

Taken by surprise, Fenn was totally unprepared for what happened next. As Dora May's heel descended toward his injured foot, Dilly's arm shot out from behind Fenn swiftly and unexpectedly, shoving Dora May backwards.

Fenn whirled around to Dilly, his mouth open in shock.

The surprised recipient of the shove was also gaping at Dilly. A group of students had begun to gather, attracted by the possibility of conflict. Someone called out, "Atta-way, Dora May, go get him!" Encouraged, she moved again to confront Fenn.

Dilly coming to the rescue once more, stepped in front of Fenn, glaring at her. "Don't you dare."

Fenn couldn't see the expression on Dilly's face but felt certain that it was fierce because another voice said, "Good for you, Dilly, she's got it coming!" Dora May backed up, thoroughly intimidated.

"Come on, Fenn," Dilly directed.

They walked out of the classroom door, but Dora May and her friend followed.

"Ah ha, Dilladora Dobson is the bodyguard of her bodyguard!" Dora May taunted. Finding great amusement at her clever quip she and her friend laughed loudly and shrilly.

Dilly, ignoring them, walked protectively by her limping body-guard, who was, she noticed, smiling broadly over the whole episode.

Out on the sidewalk, the concern that Dilly had shown him fled as quickly as she did, walking rapidly toward her next class across campus.

Shuffling along as fast as he could while trying to keep the house slipper on, Fenn became more and more irritated at himself for not buying new slippers before now. Finally arriving at the building where the dreaded child psychology class was being taught, he went in and down the hall.

When he opened the door of the classroom, he found the class in progress. Mrs. Resnick, who hadn't noticed him before, did so now.

"Yes, may I help you?"

"I uh...am just sitting in today."

"Do you have a permission slip?"

"No." He waited for Dilly to introduce him as her bodyguard—but she just gazed at him, smiling impishly.

One thing was clear to Fenn, the war was still on, and here he was—wounded. Since he wasn't good at standing, with or without a sore toe, he looked around for an empty chair to drag out into the hall. There was none.

"Will you please leave, young man," Mrs. Resnick ordered.

"Gladly." He headed for the door, but stopped, turned around and said, "After attending your class on Wednesday, I decided my mother could teach you a few things about child psychology."

Mrs. Resnick spluttered, "You...you attended my last class without permission?"

Stepping quickly out in the hall, he shut the door before she had time to build up a head of steam. Aware that he fully deserved her wrath, he decided retreat was the better part of valor.

Resigned to the fact that he had to sit on the floor, he used his knees as a resting place for his small note book and began writing. The time flew and before he realized it, the hour was over. The door opened and the class poured out. By the time he put his note book and pen back into his pocket and struggled to stand, Dilly was gone.

"Blast it!" he muttered, as he began shuffling and limping as fast as he could toward the cafeteria. Arriving there, he looked around. No Dilly. He walked around searching, then in deference to his aching toe, sat down to rest in an empty booth. He studied Dilly's schedule.

"Monday, Wednesday and Friday are supposed to be the same schedule," he whispered to himself. "Tuesday and Thursday must be the same. Something is different here, though. Boy, this is confusing—I know! Wednesday to Medford city to get some kind of form approved at the Medford City Consortium Building—I don't think that is the usual schedule. She probably won't be going there Friday, which is today. She's gone home—of course! I think I've got it now. The schedule this week on Monday and Friday *is* the same."

"You don't have to talk to yourself, you can talk to me," said a smiling attractive dark-haired girl, setting down her tray and scooting into the booth across from him. "Oh." He laughed. "I'm doing a lot of that lately. Thanks, I'd rather talk to you than to myself, but I do have to go. Could you tell me where a phone booth is?"

"Well—yes, right over there."

"Thank you." Sliding out of the booth, he left behind an obviously disappointed young lady. He shuffled over to the phone and called a taxi. Since he was still without a bus schedule he didn't want to sit at the bus stop and guess what time one would come along to take him home.

The taxi let him off around by his place. Immediately, he headed for the house hoping he was right—that Dilly was home. Then he realized the bus was slower than the taxi; she wouldn't be here yet. Just the same, he decided to check. Max wasn't anywhere around the yard, so he went into the kitchen. No Sophie. Limping to the dining room then to the library, he found no one around—downstairs anyway.

Surely, going up stairs would be invading the family's privacy—but he had to do his job. Upstairs, he looked down the wide hallway in both directions and saw four doors. It was against the contract to go into Dilly's room, but he could knock on her door, if he knew which door that was. It must be the one closest to the stairs, he decided, because she seemed to come rather quickly when called. He took the chance and knocked. Almost immediately it opened a crack.

"Dunley!" exclaimed Dilly, surprised.

"Dillweed!" exclaimed Fenn, relieved.

"How did you get here so fast?" she asked.

"How did you?"

"I asked you first."

"How else do we come and go? A taxi."

She laughed. "How clever of you to know I had come home." The words were a compliment but the sarcastic tone was not.

"How did *you* get here so fast?" he insisted.

"A friend brought me."

"Oh."

Suddenly a thought struck Dilly. One shocked look at her room ought to be enough to scare anyone away, especially Fenn. "Would you like to come in?" she asked innocently. As soon as the words were out, she regretted them. She didn't want him to see her room after all! Reminding herself she really did intend to turn over a new leaf, she reluctantly drew the door wide.

Fenn's eyes traveled around the room, certain that if a tornado had hit, it couldn't have looked worse. Quickly recovering, a broad grin spread across his face. "You live in a mighty comfortable manner, Dilly."

This wasn't the reaction she expected from this neat-freak! She lifted one eyebrow. Fenn watched as a smile began to tug at the corners of her mouth, and an amused sparkle danced in her eyes. Here we go again, he thought, as the smile turned to giggles and the giggles to help-less laughter. Plopping herself down on the cluttered bed, her hand reached out.

Without thinking, Fenn reached into his pocket, pulled out a hanky and started into the room. Suddenly remembering the contract, he stopped, one foot hanging in mid air. Recoiling, he threw the handker-chief to the floor in front of her instead. She stared at it, then glanced up, tears rolling down her cheeks, nose running, she asked innocently, "Wh... what?"

"I'm not going to get fired by stepping into your room. Besides," he grinned, "I can't find a place to step."

Picking up the ever-ready hanky, she blew her nose thoroughly.

"I'm getting low on hankies."

This started another round of hilarity. When it had abated, she blew her nose again. "Sorry, I threw them away," she said as she dropped the latest one into the overflowing waste basket beside the bed.

"But they can be washed!" he exclaimed.

"Washed? Ugh!"

"How else would they get clean?"

More laughter. When it at last subsided, the nose needed more tend-ing.

Fenn shrugged his shoulders. "Sorry, I only carry one."

She giggled. "Leave, Dunley."

"I can't, I have to find out what your plans are for this afternoon."

"I plan to study all afternoon; just leave."

"Good. And uh...you might clean your room too."

Dilly jumped up and slammed the door in his face. He laughed and continued laughing as he limped down the stairs and into the kitchen where he began foraging for something to eat.

# Chapter Ten

After doing his wash and writing a column on the perils of teaching child psychology, Fenn turned his attention to an approaching dilemma. It was Friday, and he didn't know what Dilly's plans were for tonight, for all day tomorrow and tomorrow night. He could hardly wait for Sunday so he could have a rest. He wondered: if he was this exhausted after only three days on the job, maybe the battle of wits would wear him out to the point he would have to quit. Ah, that surely did sound good. Since he was into thinking about setting records, he could set the record for being the first of Dillardora's bodyguards to *quit*! He smiled at the thought of it. How peaceful and easy his life was before he got involved with Dilladora Dobson. Though somewhat boring—it was most definitely peaceful.

The phone rang. It was Isadora.

"Fenn, we'll be eating early tonight—in five minutes to be exact."

"Thanks, Isadora, I'll be right down."

Crossing from the garage, Fenn was glad to see that they were eating on the veranda again.

"Good evening, Isadora."

"Good evening, Fenn. How is your toe?"

"The house slipper gave me more grief than the toe. It was difficult to keep it on while trying to keep up with Dilly. In fact I didn't keep up with her."

"You didn't?"

"No, but each time I lost her, I found her."

"Good."

"Good evening, everyone," Dilly greeted them, walking toward the table. Fenn noticed that she was still in the jeans and shirt she had changed into after school. This time, however, he noticed how they accentuated her slim, but very shapely figure.

Pleased to see that Sophie and Max were eating with them tonight, Fenn hoped their presence might forestall the questions Isadora had a penchant for asking.

The dinner was excellent as usual. Fenn complimented Sophie, asked Max about some gardening tips and told them about the big garden his family always raised in order to feed their family of ten. They were eating the dessert of blueberry pie when Isadora spoke up.

"How was your day, Dilly?"

"Well...it would have been good except for...oh, never mind." This instantly piqued Isadora's curiosity.

"Except for what, Dilly?" she pressed.

Dilly sighed and shook her head, putting on an exaggerated expression of concern, and stated, "Dunley insulted poor Mrs. Resnick, my child psychology teacher—in front of the whole class."

Fenn was momentarily stupefied. He didn't think Dilly liked Mrs. Resnick any more than he did. Then he laughed.

"As if you care about poor Mrs. Resnick being insulted."

"Oh, but she was so flustered, Aunt Issy," Dilly explained with gravity. "She could hardly continue her lecture."

"Your sympathy touches me—right here," Fenn said, slapping his chest.

Max and Sophie listened intently to the exchange, their heads swiveling back and forth between the combatants. Max smiled and Sophie's eyes were aglow with curiosity. "Is this true, Fenn?" Isadora asked in a serious tone of voice.

"Yes," he admitted.

"Why?"

"Her class is a joke. I was rude, I admit, but given the same circumstances, I'm sure I'd say it again."

"See, Aunt Issy, he's a trouble maker—you need to can him."

A "Hmph!" erupted from Sophie, expressing her disagreement. Max only chuckled.

"Dilladora, I can't do that unless I hear all the details. Tell me, everything, Fenn."

Fenn groaned. "It's a long story...it goes back to the first class on Wednesday." He sighed. "Maybe it would be easier if you just canned me."

Dilly giggled, but Isadora retained her serious demeanor, and demanded, "Tell me, Fenn."

Why did he hate telling these details when he loved to write them? he asked himself. For that matter, he loved telling a good story—so why? He knew of course. Having his job on the line inhibited his style. Sucking in a voluminous breath then blowing it out, he began the narrative, determined to tell only those details pertinent to Isadora's question. Soon, however, the story teller in him took over, embellishing Dilly's disagreement with Mrs. Resnick on Wednesday, and how unfeeling she was today walking ahead so fast he couldn't keep up, what with his swollen and throbbing toe. This caused him to limp into class alone after it had started, eliciting Mrs. Resnick's questioning, irritation and his final banishment. Dilly tried to refrain from giggling without much success. Fenn paused, then recounted what he had said to 'poor Mrs. Resnick.'

Everyone was silent, waiting for Isadora's reaction. For what seemed an extremely long time she studied Fenn. Finally raising her eyebrows quizzically, she asked, "You really said that?"

"Yes Ma'am, I'm afraid so."

This time it was Isadora who laughed. Max and Sophie joined in, making it a somewhat unharmonious trio. Fenn, smiling, noted that Dilly's laughing attacks not only stemmed from Obadiah, but also from these three. He dutifully pulled out a clean, neatly pressed white hanky and handed it to Isadora, mentally making a note that he needed to replenish his supply.

"Thank you, Fenn," she said, and wiped her nose genteelly, quite unlike her niece, he noted.

Dilly was not the least bit surprised at her aunt's reaction to that exaggerated story of Fenn's. After all, the part about Mrs. Resnick was delectably humorous. Nevertheless, her pride demanded that she repeat her request.

"Well, Aunt Issy, are you going to get rid of Fenn Dinkle? Our reputation at the University depends on it, I assure you," she stated emphatically, but unfortunately without much conviction.

"What do you think, Dilladora?"

"That you're going to keep him on," she replied indignantly.

"Of course, and what's more, I'm going to give him another raise."

"Can you believe this, Max?" she said, appealing to her usual ally.

"Leave me out of it, Dilly girl," Max said grinning.

"How about you, Sophie?" Dilly asked in desperation.

"I believe it," was her noncommittal reply.

"Aren't you going to ask *me*, Dilly?" queried Fenn.

"Can *you* believe it?"

"No, I can't," he laughed.

"Is there any more pie, Sophie?" Dilly asked in a sulky voice.

"Yes."

"I'll get it," Max offered.

"What time are you going out tonight, Miss Dilly?" asked Sophie.

"Sophie!" exclaimed Dilladora, glaring at her.

Fenn came alive. "You're going out? What time? Where?"

Dilly kept glaring at Sophie, who seemed very unconcerned as she finished her pie.

"Would you please tell me?" repeated Fenn.

"I have a date."

"A date?" He groaned.

"Don't worry, Dunley, you don't have to come along."

Fenn looked imploringly at Isadora for help.

"Excuse me everyone," Isadora said, getting up from her chair, "I have some business to take care of in the library."

Watching her walk off, Fenn felt a sudden touch of panic.

Sophie got up. "Excuse me, Mr. Fenn, Dilly."

"You are not excused, Sophie," Dilly said, still ruffled. "I just may not help you with the dishes tonight."

"That's all right, I'll help her, Dilly girl," Max said, placing another piece of pie in front of her. "I brought another piece for you too, Fenn."

"No thanks, Max," Fenn said, "I just lost my appetite."

Max removed the pie, gathered a few dishes and returned to the kitchen.

"If you don't tell me, Dilly, I'll camp at the bottom of the stairs and I'll find out anyway."

"Do you own a tuxedo, Dunley?"

"No, Dillweed, I don't go in for tuxedos."

"I guess you can't go then. This is a very formal affair held at the Hudson mansion. Sarah Hudson is giving one of the year's most important formal dinner dances tonight."

"Dinner...dance? You just ate dinner."

"I know. I always eat dinner before. Everyone has cocktails for hours before dinner it seems and I get too hungry if I don't eat before."

"Is your aunt attending the function?"

"No, she dislikes these kinds of socials."

"A woman after my own heart!" He groaned again. "Uh...why is this dinner dance so important?"

"Because the Hudsons are giving it, and..." she continued with extravagant emphasis, "they're one of the wealthiest and most prominent families in the city—and besides," she smiled conspiratorially, "the feast they put on is wonderful. I like to go just for the food," she confessed. "Too bad you don't own a tuxedo."

"I'll wear my Sunday suit."

"That's not acceptable...and look at your foot," she stated triumphantly.

"I won't be trying to impress anyone."

"You are not invited, Dunley."

"What did your other bodyguards do?" he implored.

"Do you really think I would answer that question?"

"No," he conceded miserably. "What time is the goon going to pick you up?"

"He's not a goon. He's a handsome young man from a very prominent family."

"What's the matter with him?"

"Why would you ask that?"

"Because at your...er...our age, the pickins' are rather slim."

"I'm not your age, Dunley," she said swallowing the last bite of pie.

"What time, Dilly?" he asked a bit more forcefully.

"Seven P.M." All sweetness now, she stood up and smiled. "Goodnight, Fenn, see you tomorrow."

He got up and gathered most of the remaining dishes, took them into the kitchen and set them on the counter.

"Thanks for the tip-off, Sophie. Could...uh you help me out a little more?"

"We've been instructed by Miss Issy..." began Sophie, regretfully. "I stepped out as it was," she finished.

"How about you, Max?"

Max smiled, but shook his head.

"Thanks anyway." He limped out of the kitchen and up to his apartment. Falling into a chair, he brooded over the upcoming evening, and wondered how in the flip he was going to do his job under the oppressive gaze of the elite of Bostonville!

# *Chapter Eleven*

At 6:45 P.M., Fenn waited for Dilly's date to arrive. His car was parked inconspicuously two brownstones up from Isadora's. He was dressed in his best Sunday suit but still had the less-than-best house slipper on—and his toe throbbed. His mood matched. After showering, he had wrapped his foot himself. Finding the bandage at first too loose, then too tight—he had complained aloud, "It didn't feel this way when Dilly did it!"

Five minutes after 7:00, Fenn watched a Rolls Royce drive up in front of Isadora's. A young man in a tuxedo got out, ran up the steps and rang the doorbell. Isadora answered it, the young man went in and the door closed behind them. Almost immediately it opened, and a gorgeous Dilly emerged with her date. Far from the casual state which was her usual attire, she had on a form-fitting, forest green, satin-like dress that flared out below the knee and ended below her ankles. It had a modest neck line with small cap sleeves. Her hair was pulled up into an exotic bun of curls, with several loose, slightly curled tendrils escaping here and there. Fenn sucked in his breath at the thoroughly captivating picture.

Fenn made a U turn and followed them for two blocks up Beacon Ave., then right two blocks to the Hudson Mansion. And, Fenn concluded, mansion it was! Cars were entering a long, wide, circular driveway in front and valets were parking the cars somewhere in back.

He parked in front on the street, and watched, trying to decide what to do next. He toyed with the idea of staying in the car until it was over, but it was very likely he'd fall asleep. On the other hand, large parties were never his style and a formal one was something to be avoided like the plague!

He watched until the guests quit coming, trying to summon the courage to go in. Finally, leaving the car where it was, he got out and reluctantly hobbled up to the driveway, then followed the curve of it to the front door.

Stepping up onto the wide covered porch with its' elegant pots of flowers on each side he stood before the beautifully carved double doors wondering if a thousand a week was enough. Deciding that it was, he reluctantly pushed the door bell and waited, dreading the evening ahead. He could hear the noise inside—people laughing and talking. Leaning against the door frame to ease his toe, he impatiently shoved the bell again just as the door opened. A stiff looking man in a butler's uniform stared at him. His eyebrows raised, he slowly perused Fenn's suit, his eyes moving downward, lingering on his slipper.

Raising his head slowly, his eyebrows still arched, he asked, "Yes? May I help you?" His voice sounded to Fenn as though it emanated from a sepulcher.

"I uh...have come to the party."

"I'm sorry, sir, but this is a formal party."

"But I am with uh..."

"Do you have an invitation?"

"Well no, but..."

"Sorry sir," he stated firmly, starting to close the door.

"Wait, I'm with Dilladora Dobson."

"Miss Dobson has already arrived with her escort," the butler said, his voice distinctly suspicious.

"But I am her new bodyguard."

"Bodyguard? Why would Miss Dobson need a bodyguard? Good night, sir!" He tried to close the door again.

"Wait! Would you do me a favor? Would you call Isadora Penbroke and verify my story?"

The man's face showed surprise at the mention of Isadora's name. "Well...all right, but you must remain outside until I do."

"Yes sir."

Minutes passed—then the door opened. The butler asked, "What is your name, sir?"

"Fenn Dinkle."

"You may come in, sir."

"Thank you," Fenn said as he stepped in.

The butler left him standing in the spacious marble-floored foyer. He looked around, hardly believing his eyes. The house was magnificent. Thirty feet away, directly in front of the door, a wide, beautiful staircase curved upward toward the high ceiling, the kind he'd only seen in the movies. He moved slowly forward, admiring it, when he heard a burst of laughter to his left. Turning, he saw a wide archway leading into a large room where groups of people were gathered, each with a small plate of food in his/her hand. Hobbling over and into the room he saw a long table, draped with a white lace table cloth, covered with a variety of platters and plates of hors d'oeuvres. One could certainly make a meal on just these Fenn mused. A quick inspection verified that Dilly was not here. Looking back across the foyer, he could see another room full of people. Surely he'd find her there. Fenn covered the distance with long, limping, purposeful strides.

The room was huge, with dim, indirect lighting all along the edges of the high ceiling. Someone somewhere was playing soft popular music on a piano. There were groups of sofas here and there with small coffee tables displaying bouquets of fresh flowers. Large valuable looking paintings hung from the walls. Indoor trees, plants, statues and large, ornately painted vases also decorated the room. People were sitting and standing in groups, all with cocktails in their hands, laughing and talking.

His eyes searched for Dilly. No luck. Several people close to him, looked up from where they were sitting and stared at him, at his attire, their eyes sliding down to his slipper. At first, there was shock, then laughter. He limped on through the archway, ignoring them. Receiving the same reaction from others as he made his way through the crowd, his sense of humor bubbled to the surface. Smiling and nodding to everyone he proceeded onward, acting as though he were the honored guest of the evening.

Finally seeing Dilly near the bar with her companion, he walked up to her.

"Good evening, Miss Dobson," he said with a friendly grin.

Her mouth dropped open, her eyes growing wide with shock, she stared at him.

"F..Fenn?"

"Yes?"

"How...how did you get in here?"

He grinned. "I walked in—or rather," he amended, "I limped in."

She looked down at his pathetic slipper and then at his suit—her mouth still open.

"Who in the hell is this man, Dilly?" asked her date, frowning in distaste at Fenn's appearance.

"Uh, he's my new bodyguard. This is Dunley Fennimore Dinkle, Dunley, this is Jim Hamilton."

"How do you do, Jim," Fenn said, holding out his hand, scrutinizing him.

Jim ignored the hand. "Dunley Fennimore Dinkle?" he snorted. "Is that a real name?"

"Would Dilly have said it if it weren't?" Fenn calmly asked.

"Well, you could at least have come in a tuxedo."

"I would have, but it wouldn't have matched my slipper," he said pointing to it.

Dilly stifled a giggle as Jim looked down. With obvious shock— then utter distaste he eyed the offending slipper. About to voice his opinion of Fenn's attire, he was interrupted by a low husky voice.

"Dilly, Jim. It's good to see you."

Fenn looked up from his slipper to see a striking blonde, dressed in an ivory colored strapless evening gown decorated in shimmering sequin flowers and pearl beads.

"Sarah, it's good to see you too," said Dilly, still struggling to keep a straight face. "I would like you to meet my new bodyguard, Dunley Fennimore Dinkle. Dunley, this is Sarah Hudson, the hostess of this regal party."

Fenn listened, amazed. Dilly's introduction held no apology or embarrassment over his presence or his lack of proper dress.

Sarah Hudson stared at Fenn in silence.

"Glad to meet you Miss Hudson. Everyone, but Dilly, calls me Fenn, short for Fennimore."

"Oh?" she said, momentarily taken back by his attire as well as his name, then her impeccable manners came to the rescue. "Uh..it is nice to meet you—Fenn, you say?"

"Yes ma'am," he answered smiling.

"May I escort you to the bar for a cocktail?"

"No, thank you, Miss Hudson, I don't drink."

"Oh." Then with the smoothness of a good hostess, she asked, "Would you like a soft drink then?"

"No, nothing thank you." It was at this moment he noted, with relief, that Dilly didn't have a drink of any kind in her hand, although her date did.

"Well, come then," Sarah said, taking his arm, "let me escort you to the hors d'oeuvres."

He hesitated, looking over at Dilly.

"Don't worry," Sarah assured Fenn. "Dilly won't be going anywhere—at least until after dinner." She smiled knowingly at Dilly then at Fenn.

"Uh...thank you, ma'am."

"Please, call me Sarah."

"Thank you, Sarah." They took a few steps, then Sarah stopped. "My goodness," she said, looking down, "you're limping."

Dilly and Jim Hamilton watched, waiting for Sarah's reaction to Fenn's startling footgear.

"What is the matter?" she asked solicitously.

"I think I broke my little toe and I can't get my shoe on."

Sarah laughed. "That slipper looks like an antique. Surely it must be valuable."

Fenn laughed. "Thanks for those kind words."

Dilly, her mouth slightly ajar, watched Sarah Hudson glom on to her bodyguard and walk off with him—and she didn't know quite what to think about it.

"Good!" her date said, interrupting her thoughts. "We won't have him around now. Let's mingle."

Fenn felt he received more than his share of attention from the hostess. He found Sarah charming and gracious. They had just finished a plate of hors d'oeuvres together in a secluded part of the room.

"You need to mingle with your guests, Sarah. You've been mighty kind to me, especially since I'm a party crasher and dressed inappropriately."

She smiled. "I guess I had better mingle. Come, I'll introduce you to some girls who have come without partners—but I reserve you as my partner when dinner is served."

"Thank you, Sarah, I would like that."

After the introductions, Fenn, surprised at the attention he received from these beautifully dressed girls without partners, admitted to himself how much he was enjoying it. It had been, he reflected, far too long since his last date.

Dilly noticed the crowd of females hovering around Fenn, one hanging on each arm. She frowned. He was supposed to be protecting me, she thought—not flirting with all those girls. Immediately, annoyed with herself, she realized that the girls were flirting with him—but he certainly looked like he was enjoying it! Watching, she had to admit that she couldn't blame the girls for hanging around him; he was tall, broad shouldered, and emanated a powerful air of masculinity. She noticed how his charismatic smile was affecting his new fan club—and felt unnerved at how it was also affecting her.

Jim Hamilton, misinterpreting Dilly's expression, sneered, "Me too, Dilly, I can't imagine what all the fuss is about."

Fenn noticed Dilly looking in his direction. He motioned her over.

"Excuse me, Jim," Dilly said, a little too eagerly. She walked over to Fenn and the group.

"Dilly, I apologize for pulling you away from your date, but I need you to rewrap my foot. I think I wrapped it too tight and my toe is throbbing."

"Sit down."

"Gladly," he said limping over to a sofa while the sympathetic group followed, 'oohing' and 'aahing' over his sore foot.

Fenn smiled as Dilladora Dobson, radiant in her beautiful green gown, knelt down in front of him, seemingly unaware of any breach of social etiquette, and calmly pulled off his dilapidated slipper. Several of the girls tittered.

Jim Hamilton walked over and glowered at Dilly, then leaned down and whispered, "You're making a fool of yourself, Dilly, and you're embarrassing me. Get up off the floor!"

Overhearing the remark, Fenn watched Dilly closely.

"Don't be ridiculous, Jim," she whispered back. "I'll be with you in a minute."

Furious, Jim stomped off.

As Dilly finished rewrapping his foot, she asked, "How does that feel?"

"Much better!" I'm obliged, Dilly. Thank you," he said.

The smile she'd suddenly become so aware of tonight, was now directed at her, making her flush uncomfortably. "I...I don't know whether you're welcome or not," she whispered. "You may have caused me to lose my date."

He leaned forward and whispered into her ear, "Not much of a loss then, if you ask me."

"I didn't ask you," she snapped. Standing up gracefully, she turned and sauntered off, her movements provocative, alluring in the form fitting dress. Fenn was enjoying the view immensely when it was blocked by the lovely, but less interesting girls who had waited patiently for Dilly to take care of his foot. They now surrounded him completely, making it impossible to see where Dilly had gone.

Dinner was served at 8:30 and Fenn, surprised that he was still hungry after eating dinner at Isadora's and hors d'oeuvres here, was looking forward to it.

Double doors, leading from the far end of the dining room, were opened revealing a large room filled with circular tables. The tables were set with white tablecloths, delicate crystal and china with fresh flowers as center pieces. Brightly lit crystal chandeliers shimmered over the guests as they seated themselves, talking and laughing loudly—a result of too many cocktails, Fenn figured. A live orchestra, composed mainly of violins, played lovely dinner music.

It amazed Fenn to see that one family had the means to put on such an outrageously expensive party.

The head table, Fenn found out, was where the hostess, her parents and a select group of friends sat. It was rectangular and everyone sat on only one side of it. Fenn wondered if this was so that the host and hostesses could keep an eye on the service their guests were receiving—or maybe it was so they could be seen by all. Probably the latter, he thought, feeling somewhat cynical about the whole affair.

Sarah's parents, appalled, disapproving and embarrassed by his presence, ignored him—at the same time allowing their daughter her foolish peccadillo.

Fenn at Sarah's right, didn't realize the honor of his position but Dilly did, and she was feeling a little disconcerted over it. As Jim had said, what was all the fuss about? True, he was good-looking and had a very unique personality, but she wasn't aware that Sarah Hudson went in for 'characters.' Sarah was known for her attraction to the smooth, handsome and wealthy—and Fenn was none of these. Sarah, twenty-nine years old, and engaged three times, fueled rumors and speculation as to who broke off the engagements.

Dilly knew all three of Sarah's ex-fiances and found them somewhat selfish, shallow and boring—and Fenn was none of these things. At least in the four days she'd known him, it certainly hadn't been the case.

But why, she asked herself, was it bothering her? Why do I care how Sarah feels about Fenn? What possible difference does it make? After all, he's just a bodyguard, and previously made a living as a weight trainer, something she did not admire in the least!

The food was everything Dilly had led him to expect, and Fenn thoroughly enjoyed both it and Sarah's conversation. The man on Sarah's left vied for her attention, but only received that which courtesy demanded, and so he had to carry on a conversation with her father instead.

Fenn could tell that he was the subject of disparaging conversation by several at the head table, as well as a couple of people at Dilly's table, which was directly in front of him. He didn't mind. After all, as an inappropriately dressed party crasher, he deserved it. There was, however, something he did mind, and that was the way Jim Hamilton was treating Dilly! Apparently still embarrassed and angry over Dilly kneeling on the floor and serving the hired help, Jim ignored her and flirted with the girl to his left. He also drank one glass of wine after another. By the time dessert came, Fenn was seething and unable to carry on a decent conversation with Sarah.

"Excuse me a moment, Sarah," he said, getting up from the table. Shuffling over to Dilly's table, he leaned down between her and Jim Hamilton and whispered to her escort.

"Excuse me, Jim, but do you remember the girl you brought tonight?"

Jim looked at him first in surprise, then in disgust. "Don't be asinine, of course I do!"

"Shh," whispered Fenn. "Not so loud, Jim, you'll make a fool of yourself."

Jim looked around uncomfortably and Fenn continued. "Then since you know who you brought, I suggest you quit flirting and give her some attention—or I'll see you outside later, and—I think you've had enough to drink."

Jim Hamilton's face turned crimson with anger.

"Shh," Fenn cautioned again. "Careful, you'll make a fool of yourself."

Fenn glanced over at Dilly and noted the fire in her blue eyes and her tightly pressed lips. He left quickly, returning to the safety of Sarah's table. Feeling much better, he continued to enjoy himself.

Dinner over with, Sarah stood up and suggested that everyone mingle in the other room while the tables were removed for the dance.

While waiting for the dining area to be turned into a ballroom, Fenn observed the continued serving of after-dinner cocktails, noting with concern that Jim Hamilton was continuing to drink.

The orchestra began playing dance music, a signal that the ballroom was ready. The guests began gravitating in that direction.

Sarah, who had been busy overseeing the clearing of the ballroom, came up to him and invited him to sit on one of the chairs bordering the dance floor and rest his foot. Thanking her, he did so, once he was certain Jim and Dilly were safely inside the ballroom dancing.

He watched them with annoyance. Jim Hamilton was holding Dilly a little too close, and—after he had treated her so badly. Relieved to see a man cut in on Jim, he relaxed and enjoyed watching the other handsomely dressed couples dance.

Sarah seemed to have many suitors, one after the other keeping her occupied on the dance floor. Fenn noticed that Dilly also had more than her share. The next time he looked, Jim had her in his arms again, slobbering over her. Not able to stand it any longer. Fenn hobbled out onto the floor.

"May I cut in?" he asked Jim.

"What? You?!" he asked in a belligerent, drunken tone.

"Just a short one, Jim, relax."

"Awright, jush a short one," he warned, his words slurring.

Fenn put his arm around Dilly's pleasantly slender body, catching his breath as the feel of her sent his senses reeling.

"Hi," he managed to say, smiling down at her.

Dilly stared up at him in disbelief. The sensation of Fenn's arm around her waist elicited a sudden intake of breath. "Fenn!" she breathed out in a gasp then added in almost a whisper, "You are not to touch me. Besides, your foot—you can't dance."

"Oh, I can shuffle a little." The orchestra was playing a soft, romantic melody. He leaned down, pressed his cheek against hers to whisper something important, but the thrill of touching her shot through him like a hot arrow. He pulled her close, forgetting what he was going to say.

Dilly, jolted by something she'd never felt before—intoxication from a man's touch, from the feel of his arms around her, from the feel of his face against hers—was stricken silent.

How long they danced like that, neither one knew. Fenn came to his senses first, realizing finally his intended mission. Reluctantly, he whispered into her ear, "It's time, Dilly."

"Time, Fenn?" she whispered back expectantly.

"Yes, it's time to go home."

"Home?" she murmured, dreamily.

"Yes, Dilly."

Dilly blinked, suddenly returning to the real world. "Fenn Dinkle!" she exclaimed, pulling away from him. "You are not my father! You are only my bodyguard!"

"Jim Hamilton is drunk and he's getting drunker and more possessive by the minute. I've seen his kind before."

"That is none of your business!"

"It *is* my business. You are not riding home with him."

"I don't intend to, I'm walking home."

"Good, but may I drive you—now?"

"No. The party's not over."

"But everyone is still drinking and since you don't drink, aren't you getting a little bored?"

"As I said, it is none of your business."

"Fenn," a low husky voice floated up to his ear, "if you can dance, how about asking me?" Sarah Hudson smiled invitingly as she and her partner danced nearby.

Fenn flushed. "I will, Sarah, but you won't enjoy my so-called dancing."

As Sarah and her partner moved away, Dilly pulled a face. "I see you've managed to intrigue *her*, along with a few others."

Just then Jim Hamilton tried to cut in. Fenn felt helpless. If it weren't for the embarrassment it would cause Sarah, he would pick Dilly up and carry her out to the car right now. The thought crossed his mind—he might need a pair of handcuffs if he did so. The music stopped and a jazz piece began.

Just as Fenn released Dilly to Jim, an exuberant couple came whirling around, bumping into Jim, upsetting his fragile equilibrium. Down he went, grabbing unsuccessfully at Dilladora for support. Trying to step over Jim's crumpled body, Dilly tripped over him and fell forward. Before she could fall to the floor, she found herself swept up into Fenn's strong arms and moved out of the way. At the same time, an inebriated couple came whirling toward their vacated spot, unaware of the obstacle on the floor—Jim, struggling to get to his knees. Tripping over him, they fell headlong onto the floor, knocking him back down, flattening his face against the hard wood of the dance floor.

Dodging the dancing couples, Fenn whisked Dilly safely to the sidelines away from the screaming, tumbling pandemonium. They watched in awe as a crowd gathered around the dazed threesome who were sprawled out on the floor in a most unbecoming arrangement.

"Whew!" Fenn gasped. "That was close." They looked at each other—silent a moment, then laughed.

"That was some maneuver you pulled off," Dilly said breathlessly, more impressed than she let on. "Thank you."

Fenn, still holding Dilly in his arms, felt his heart thumping against his chest more vigorously than the exertion warranted. He grinned and breathed out, "You're welcome, anytime."

Dilly waited for him to put her down—something Fenn didn't seem in any hurry to do. Disturbed that her heart was pounding furiously, she said, "You may put me down now."

"To tell the truth, I'm seriously considering carrying you out to my car and driving you home."

"Fenn Dinkle, put me down this instant."

He grinned. "What if I say no."

"If you say that, I'll tell Aunt Issy on you."

"All right, if you put it that way," he said, reluctantly putting her down.

Just at that moment, a stumbling, disheveled, red-nosed Jim Hamilton came toward them. "Where'd ya go, Dilly. Someone knocked me down. C'mon le's dance."

Without a backward glance, Dilly went with him, disappearing into the dancing crowd. Fenn stood there glowering, feeling angry and frustrated that the young woman he'd just rescued went right back into the arms of danger!

"Why are you looking so grim, Fenn?" Sarah asked as she walked up to him.

"Oh, hello, Sarah," he said, trying to pull his thoughts away from Dilly. "It sounds like the orchestra is playing a slow one, so how about that dance?"

She smiled. "Why do you think I'm here?" she said, going into his arms.

"I warn you, Sarah. It's not much fun to do my brand of 'the shuffle.'"

"That's all right, Fenn." Much shorter than Dilly, Sarah put her arm across his back and laid her face upon his chest, pulling him close. Alcohol, it seemed, had also loosened Sarah's inhibitions making him feel more than a little uncomfortable.

Luckily for him, the next dance was a fast one. "I'll have to sit this one out, Sarah."

"All right, Fenn. I'll sit it out with you," she said, her voice seductive.

As they walked toward the sidelines, Fenn was starting to sweat when a young man rescued him by asking Sarah to dance. It was a prospect, Fenn felt, that did not please her, but he watched her innate graciousness take over as she accepted the young man's invitation.

Feeling worn out and edgy, he found an out-of-the-way spot, hoping not to be seen by another female, then watched for Dilly the best he could.

Checking his watch, he saw that it was eleven-forty-five and wondered wearily how late this party was going to last. He glanced up just in time to catch a glimpse of Dilly walking rapidly out of the ballroom, followed by Jim Hamilton. Fenn jumped up and pushed his way through the dancing crowd. Entering the dining room, he saw they weren't there. Half shuffling, half hopping, he moved as swiftly as possible through the dining room, and across the wide foyer to the large sitting room, almost losing his slipper in the process. Looking around, he saw a few couples at the bar and a few seated visiting, but no Dilly. He moved quickly back through the foyer and out the front door, his slipper dangling precariously from the swollen toe. Relief flooded through him as he caught sight of her out on the driveway directly in front of the porch. He stopped, remaining on the porch, listening and watching while readjusting his slipper.

Jim Hamilton had a grip on Dilly's shoulders. "Let go of me, Jim," Dilly demanded. "You're drunk." .

"No I'm not, I jus wanna lil' kiss."

Fenn knew Dilly could handle it herself if he could just hold back.

"Let go of me, you drunken bum!"

Anger contorted his face. "That does it!" he growled pulling her roughly to him.

Tearing herself out of his grasp, she turned to run, but he lunged for her, grabbing the back of her dress, ripping it.

Before Jim Hamilton knew what was happening, Fenn had grabbed his shoulder, and swung him around.

Startled, Jim blurted out, "What the h...."

"The lady doesn't want your attention!"

Dilly, stopped running and turned, glaring at the two men, furious at both.

Fueled by contempt and a desire for retaliation, Hamilton swung at Fenn who adroitly dodged the blow.

Stumbling toward Fenn, Jim Hamilton swung like a windmill, one blow after another, all unsuccessful.

Realizing that Hamilton's drunken rage was not going to permit a discussion, Fenn doubled up his fist and landed a blow to the jaw, propelling him backwards onto the ground.

Dilly stared at Fenn and then at her date who lay groaning on the ground. Turning away from both, she ran down the driveway, through the gate and out onto the sidewalk.

Fenn hobbled after her. "Dilly, let me drive you!"

"No!" she yelled. Stopping to take off her shoes, she lifted her skirt and ran.

Fenn found his car, got in and drove alongside her, slowing down when she did, speeding up when she did, until she was home and safely to the door. She rummaged through her small purse and apparently unable to find the key, rang the doorbell. The door soon opened. Apparently Isadora had been waiting up. Fenn waved at her and drove around to his place, wondering what she would think of Dilly's torn dress. He also wondered if he was going to survive one more week of this business of guarding the...the most contrary, the most difficult girl he'd ever known!

# Chapter Twelve

Fenn woke up at 6:30 A.M., perspiring and exhausted. When totally awake, he contemplated the dream that had caused him so much tossing and turning. All night, it seemed, he had tried to swim a dark moat to reach the castle and rescue the princess. Try as he would, his frantic strokes didn't move him forward an inch. The odd thing about the dream was—the princess didn't know she was in danger, she just laughed and waved from a high turret window. Fenn chuckled at the dream. After last night, no wonder!

He jumped out of bed, realizing immediately that his toe was feeling much better. "It couldn't have been broken," he muttered as he walked into the front room and looked out the window. It was a beautiful morning. He noticed Max digging in a bed of flowers and wondered if he could use some help. Finding an old shirt and a pair of jeans, he dressed quickly. He decided that a thick sock and his old ragged tennis shoes might take care of the toe just fine.

Once outside, he moved quickly over to where Max was working in the flower bed. "Good morning, Max."

"Why good morning, Fenn. You're up early after a night of partying."

"Can I help?"

"You bet," Max answered, handing him a small three pronged tool. "The soil needs to be loosened around these flowers so that I can add fertilizer. How did it go last night?"

Fenn laughed. "I broke a few conventions. I attended a formal party of the elite of Bostonville, uninvited, in just a suit, and—in my tattered house slipper."

Max stopped sprinkling the fertilizer over the soil and looked at him. "You actually went in?"

"Yep."

Max slapped his knee and laughed. "That's good, now that's good!"

Fenn stared at him in surprise. "You mean the other bodyguards didn't go into the parties?"

"Nope."

Fenn thought about this a minute. "Well, just because Dilly is inside, it doesn't mean that all is well."

As they worked, Fenn became aware that Isadora and Dilly had come out onto the veranda. He waved, receiving a response only from Isadora. It was obvious that Dilly was still out of sorts.

They worked until eight, then Max suggested they stop for breakfast.

"Thanks for the help, Fenn."

"Thanks for letting me, it felt good."

Max went on into the kitchen and Fenn walked up onto the veranda where Dilly and Isadora were engrossed in the morning paper.

"Good morning, you two," he said smiling.

"Good morning, Fenn," Isadora said. "I see you were helping Max."

"Yes, it's a beautiful morning. I enjoyed it. How are you this morning?"

"I'm very well, Fenn, thank you."

"And you, Dilly?"

She ignored him, continuing to read.

Unfazed by Dilly's lack of manners, he asked, "Have you both had breakfast?"

"No," Isadora replied. "We were waiting for you and Max."

"Do you think Sophie would mind if I wash up in the kitchen?"

"Max does it all the time. That's probably what he's doing right now."

Fenn came back after washing up, and sat down. "What is so interesting in the paper this morning?"

Dilly and Isadora glanced at each other.

"You really want to know, Dunley?"

"Uh oh, that tells me something doesn't bode well. Maybe I don't."

Dilly shoved the paper at him, opening it up so that he could see the two page review of the Hudson dinner party, replete with pictures. The headline stunned him. "INTERLOPER CRASHES HUDSON GALA OF THE YEAR!" There was a full length picture of him that included his slipper—then a close up of it!

"How...how did they get this picture? I didn't see anyone taking pictures." There were more. One of him surrounded by girls, one dancing with Sarah Hudson and one sitting at her table. Apparently, he thought with relief, no one noticed me carrying Dilly off the dance floor.

He frowned. "Why...they're treating me like...like I was the star of the show!" he finally exclaimed.

"Oh you were, Dunley. You most definitely were."

Thoroughly shocked, he began reading the somewhat lurid and overblown account which appeared under the by-line of the society editor, a well-known arbiter of local taste.

> "And who was this party crasher? No less than the latest in a long line of Dilladora Dobson's bodyguards. The man had the audacity to push his way in, dressed informally and with a most reprehensible covering for his lame foot— would you believe an old ragged house slipper? Miss Sarah Hudson, the hostess of the grand and regal function, handled it in her usual kind and gracious manner.
>
> Dilladora Dobson, the niece of Isadora Penbroke and the late Obadiah Penbroke III, the wealthy and prominent benefactors of the City of Bostonville, seemed astonished that this yeoman had managed to maneuver his way in. But did she escort him out? No. Dobson, well known by all for her flamboyant disregard of the social civilities that one in her station should adhere to, followed her usual 'march to a different drummer.' She allowed him to remain—causing obvious discomfort to many of the guests.

At one point early in the evening, Dobson displayed her lack of decorum even further by kneeling on the floor before the uncouth young man and rewrapping his foot. Jim Hamilton, her escort—a member of the prominent Hamilton family of Bostonville—embarrassed by her improper conduct, tried unsuccessfully to dissuade her

And what was the name of this interloper? Dunley Fennimore Dinkle. A real name? Believe it or not, it is. It also happens to be the name of my fellow columnist here on the paper who writes under the title of "Human Nature at it's Best" which comes out now and then in both, the Bostonville Globe and the Medford City times. Is Dunley Fennimore Dinkle living a double life?

What was Dinkle really doing there? It certainly did not look like he was there to guard the beautiful red head since he was at various times surrounded by a group of local beauties, or wooing the lovely Sarah Hudson.

However, he did try to do his 'job' at one point in the evening—to the chagrin of the gracious hostess. Two hours before the formal function was over, Dobson was seen running out the front door with Hamilton following. Dinkle finally came to, and followed them out (in his limping fashion). The valets reported that there was an argument between Hamilton and Dobson. Dinkle, it seemed, wanting to look like a hero in the eyes of the wealthy but fiery red head, decked Hamilton, knocking him to the ground in the middle of the driveway. Dobson, it was reported, ran down the driveway with Dinkle following. One can only guess what happened after that."

Fenn skimmed the rest of the two pages, finding, thankfully, only boring details of the party. Still trying to comprehend himself as the object of society gossip, he gazed at Isadora and Dilly. Both had sober expressions on their faces.

"I can't believe all this," he said, shaking his head. Then the ludicrous nature of it all hit him full force. "I can't believe it!" His amusement escalated, his body shook with laughter. Quite a few moments later, he pulled out a neatly pressed hanky for himself. When at last he regained a tenuous control, he asked, "I'm fired?"

Isadora, still not smiling, asked, "How did you feel about that party last night, Fenn?"

"I'll put it this way...I'm going to avoid another one like I would the plague!"

To Fenn's surprise, Dilly and Isadora burst out laughing. Apparently they'd been struggling to hold back their own amusement. As Dilly's hilarity subsided, she blew her nose unceremoniously on a paper napkin and Isadora likewise but with much more ladylike finesse.

"Why didn't you tell me you were a columnist, Dunley?"

Fenn looked at Dilly in surprise. "How would I know you were interested in knowing that? Anyway, it isn't much to brag about. The papers only put my column in when they don't know what else to do with the space."

"Well, it so happens that the paper decided to put your column in today. I wonder why? Could it be that you've become an infamous celebrity?"

"You saw my column?"

"I did more than that, I read it."

"Oh?"

"Yes, it's uh..."

Fenn found himself anxious to know her opinion, but said lightly, "Go ahead, Dilly, I can take it on the chin."

"It's uh...well...clever, interesting."

"Well, I'll be darned, Dillweed, I never expected a compliment from you."

Sophie came out with a cart full of breakfast which occupied their attention for some time.

"How did you get into journalism, Dunley?" asked Dilly, munching on a sweet roll, trying to seem only casually interested.

"Oh—I studied some journalism in college and I've done some free lance writing."

"Go on," prodded Isadora, "tell the whole story."

"Well.." said Fenn evasively, "there really isn't much more to tell."

Isadora remarked impatiently, "There was more to the story when you first recounted it to me. Now—let's hear it."

"Well—I can't see who could possibly be interested," he said glancing at Dilly, then back to Isadora. "But all right if you insist, he began, looking only at Isadora, "I studied computer science, got a Masters degree in business, developed my own software business, sold it and intend to use the profit toward a business I'm more interested in. Is that what you wanted, Isadora?"

"That will do, Fenn, at least for the time being."

For an interval of time, Dilly was silent, digesting the information. Yes, she thought, a few incongruous and puzzling things about Fenn made sense now.

"All right," she said at last, "so I have an educated and cerebral bodyguard. Surely, Aunt Issy, you don't think that will make me tolerate having him around any better? I still want you to fire him. Remember how much trouble he caused at poor Sarah's party."

"You're beginning to sound like a broken record, Dilladora."

Dilly's frustration mounted. "But, Aunt Issy, he's gone far beyond just being a bodyguard, he's...he's acting like a...a big brother! You know Jim Hamilton and how he lives the letter of the law when it comes to being socially correct?"

"Yes."

"Well, as it said in the paper, I embarrassed him when I knelt down and rewrapped Fenn's foot, so he was trying to get back at me by flirting with the girl on his left."

"That doesn't sound socially correct in my book, Dilly," commented Fenn.

"He was drinking."

"Oh, that excuses it?"

"No, but you stay out of it, Fenn Dinkle! Aunt Issy, I had already decided to never date him again."

"You should have walked out on him right then," stated Fenn emphatically.

"See? It's just like I told you, he's interfering and acting like a big brother!"

"Go on with your story, Dilly," stated Isadora calmly.

"Well, Mr. Dunley-do-Right here, leaves Sarah Hudson's table and comes over to my table, and leans over between Jim and me and whispers so I can hear, I'm sure. He had the nerve to ask Jim if he remembered who he brought to the party."

Isadora smiled thinly. "I'm sure that irked, Jim."

"And then, he told him to quit flirting with that girl, or he'd see him outside later. Now if that doesn't sound like an interfering, overprotective big brother, I don't know what does."

"You've always wanted a big brother, Dilly," remarked her aunt.

Dilly stood up, incensed. "Aunt Isadora, he's *not* my brother. He's a...he's an *interloper*!'" She turned and walked off in a huff.

# Chapter Thirteen

After breakfast, Fenn showered and dressed in jeans and a casual shirt. He was trying to decide if he dared leave and do a little shopping, when he heard a knock at the door. Startled, he opened it. The last person he expected to see on his doorstep was Dilladora. Nevertheless, there she was, still dressed as he saw her at breakfast, in the attractively snug jeans and bright blue T shirt the color of her eyes.

"Hey, Dilly! This is a pleasant surprise. No one ever visits me up here in my little pad."

"Ever? You've only been here four days, Dunley."

"Only four days? You mean I've only been on the job four days? It seems like four weeks."

"It seems like four months to me."

"Come on in, Dilly."

"I have some letters here for you. They came this morning," she said, stepping inside.

Fenn's face brightened. "Great, they've answered already. But...don't I have a private mail box?"

"No," she said. "And I'm the official mail getter—so I get to be nosey and look at it carefully before I turn it over to you."

"Checking on me, huh?" He reached for the mail but she put it behind her back.

"I want you to answer some questions first."

"Oh? Well, do have a seat then, Miss Dobson, we might as well be comfortable while I hear these questions."

Dilly sat down and looked at the mail in her hand. "You certainly got a bundle from your family. How could you write and get an answer back so quickly?"

"I have a fax machine and I bought one for my folks."

"Why didn't they fax back?"

Fenn chuckled. "My parents are still a little intimidated by the machine, I'm afraid, but they'll catch on to the convenience of it one of these days."

"Well, let's see," Dilly said, looking at Fenn's mail. "There is one from Mr. and Mrs. Hans Dinkle, one from Emmiline and John, one from Andy Dinkle and one from Willie Dinkle."

"Aren't you infringing upon my privacy, Dilladora?"

"Aren't you infringing on mine?"

"Yes, but I'm getting paid for it, you aren't."

"No matter, two of your brothers have written something on the back of their letters that I'm curious about."

"Good Grief, I'll have to tell them not to do that again—or use the fax. What did they say?"

"The letter from someone named Andy says: 'P.S. Hey, is Isadora Penbroke blind?'"

Fenn laughed. "That is a jibe from my fifteen-year-old brother about my long, lanky physique. I knew it was coming."

"Oh." Dilly smiled. "I agree with Andy. Aunt Issy must be blind to hire you as a bodyguard."

"You mean, you can't tell if I'm noticeably bulked up, even after all the weight lifting I've done?"

Dilly was surprised. He was serious. "Am I supposed to?" she teased.

"Yes. I thought it might improve my chances with the girls," he said, disappointment in his voice.

"You seemed to do all right with the girls last night."

"I always impress the ones I don't care about impressing."

"For what it's worth, and I'm sure it won't be worth much coming from me, but tell Andy that I like your physique."

Fenn's face brightened, feeling more pleased than he wanted to admit. "You do?"

The phone rang. "Excuse me, Dilly, it must be your aunt. Hello?" Fenn flushed and glanced over at Dilly. "Oh hello, Sarah, how are you?....Yes I saw the paper. I'm sorry I caused such an uproar at your nice party last night"....Seeing the little smirk on Dilly's face as she listened to the conversation, he pretended to enjoy his visit with Sarah. "Yes, Dilladora is fine," he said, all smiles. Have you heard how

Hamilton is?....Good....Oh....uh, Sarah, thank you, but my job includes evenings too....Just when Dilladora goes out....I haven't checked with her about this evening but I....What?....All right, I'll find out and call you back....What is your number?" Fenn, taking the ever ready pen and notebook from his shirt pocket, jotted down the number.... "All right, thank you for calling, Sarah."

Dilly felt irritated. "She asked you out tonight?"

"Yes. She has two tickets to a concert." Then after a pause added hopefully, "You *are* going out tonight aren't you?"

Dilly snickered, realizing that Fenn didn't want to go after all. "If I remember right, you were relieved when I've said I wasn't going out. Now you want me to?"

"Yes."

"Sarah Hudson is beautiful and nice," she said, wanting his reaction.

"Yes, I agree...but...uh she doesn't really know me. How does she know that I'm not a fortune hunter like they insinuated in the paper?"

"Are you?"

Fenn grinned. "That's it, I'll tell her that I am."

"That won't deter her, she's had her share of those and continues to date them even when she knows."

"Oh. Well, *are* you going out tonight, Dilly?"

"I'll answer that question after you answer mine."

"All right."

"Who is Willie?"

"He's my thirteen-year-old brother."

"On the back of Willie's letter, he asks: 'What kind of a spider was on the pencil you gave Miss Justin?' I didn't know anything about a spider. Did you do that?"

"Yes I gave her a pencil with a spider on it."

"Why?"

"I answered your question, now you answer mine."

"No."

"You only bargained for one question and that is your third one which I'm not going to answer."

"Then I'm not going to tell you if I'm going out tonight."

"Okay...fine." He picked up the phone and dialed Sarah Hudson. "Sarah, this is Fenn."

Dilly's mouth tightened in frustration.

"I'm sorry, but I won't be able to go with you tonight. I can't find out if Dilladora is going out or not....You do?....They do?....Well, you understand my predicament then. Thank you for asking me....Yes, maybe there will be another time, and thank you for being so gracious to me after I crashed your party." .... Fenn laughed .... "It did? .... Good .... well, I had better get back to my job. Thank you again, Sarah, goodbye."

"What did she say about me?" Dilly demanded.

"That would be divulging."

"Tell me about the spider."

Fenn, now realized curiosity was Dilly's Achilles heel. Maybe he could use it to his advantage sometime.

"Did you do it for revenge?"

Fenn smiled. "No, I didn't do it for revenge."

"Then why?"

"You're wasting your time, Dilly."

She pouted for a moment, then surprised Fenn by asking the names of all his siblings. He was happy to answer that question.

"I am the oldest. I have a sister two years younger, twenty-eight, named Emmeline. She is married to John and they have three little girls. The next is a sister named Lavinnia, and she is your age, twenty-seven and married to Jack. They have two little girls. My sister, Cecelia is twenty-five. She is married to Dave and has a baby boy. Then there's my brother, Frederick who's twenty-three. He and my twenty-one-year-old brother, Chester, are attending college. The only ones home now are Andy and Willie."

Dilly, still holding the letters, stared at them, silent for a moment, then said in a detached tone of voice, "I've always wondered what it would be like to have brothers and sisters."

"I could take you to meet them some weekend," he blurted out impulsively. "They live in a lush valley only four hours from here. In fact, all my family are on the edge of their seats over my new job. They would love to meet the beautiful Dilladora Dobson who I'm guarding with my life."

"Really?" Dilly looked at him wistfully for a moment. "That's a very nice offer. I wish I could accept."

"Why can't you?" he asked, feeling disappointed.

"I'm sure you can figure it out," she said standing up and handing him the letters.

"Well, then, Dilly, how about riding with me to buy a couple of newspapers."

"You want that article?"

"Yes, one for my memoirs and one for my family. They'll fall off their chairs when they read it."

"I imagine so," she chuckled.

"Will you go with me? Then, I would like you to accompany me to the store to buy some more white hankies—and help me choose a new pair of house slippers."

"I like your old ones."

"Good, then I won't buy a new pair."

"Your toe! I forgot about your toe. How is it?" She glanced down seeing it now housed in an old worn tennis shoe.

"Much better, thanks to your tender care. Are you coming with me to buy the newspapers and hankies?"

Smiling slyly, she stepped to the door. "So that you can keep track of me, Dunley? Thanks, but no thanks." She opened the door and scurried out and down the steps.

Fenn hollered down after her. "Are you going out this afternoon or tonight?"

Turning, she looked up and grinned. "Wouldn't you like to know?"

# Chapter Fourteen

In the kitchen, Fenn dogged Sophie's steps. He'd been watching the stairs for Dilly, so concerned that she might try to sneak out that he had not dared even to go buy the newspapers. He had to ask Max if he'd do that favor for him. It was 3:00 P.M. Frustrated and still in the dark concerning Dilly's plans, he tried once more to pry it out of Sophie.

"Even if I knew, Mr. Fenn," stated Sophie, "as I've said before, I've been instructed to stay out of it. All I know is that Dilly could very well have a date. She goes through young men like Max goes through raisin cookies." Sophie turned, nearly bumping into him as she headed toward the refrigerator. "She usually won't date one young man more than two or three times and then she turns down more than she dates." Fenn stepped out of her way as Sophie walked to the sink with an armful of vegetables. "Just when we all think there couldn't be another young man in the whole county, another one comes out of the woodwork. I've never seen the like," she said, shaking her head. "I just wish the right one would come along so she'd settle down and quit worrying her aunt."

"Thanks anyway, Sophie," he mumbled walking out of the kitchen toward the library. Entering it, he chose a book, picked up one of the smaller chairs, parked himself at the bottom of the stairs and began reading.

Thirty minutes later, Dilly came running down the steps and stopped midway. "Dunley!" she shrieked. "You are absolutely the biggest pest Aunt Issy has hired yet! None of them stuck to me like crazy glue the way you do."

"My father always taught us—'if you have a job,'" he grinned, "'stick to it.'"

Ignoring the pun, she descended to the foyer and stepped around him, heading toward the front door. Fenn quickly moved ahead of her and blocked the door.

"Where are we going?" he asked.

Her voice rose. *"We* are going nowhere. *I* am going somewhere."

Fenn noticed how lovely she looked in the pale yellow silk dress with gold earrings and bracelet. Her hair was slightly curled, loose and shiny. Her delicate perfume unsettled him as he remembered how she felt in his arms the night before.

Shaking the memory away, he looked down at his jeans, unpressed shirt and scruffy tennis shoes and said, "I guess I'm not dressed for the occasion."

"So what else is new?"

"If you could tell me in advance, I could dress in more fitting attire."

"It so happens that it would be impossible on this occasion. Men are not invited. I'm going to a baby shower."

Fenn's face lit up. "A baby shower? I love baby showers. My mother always took me along when I was a boy so I could tend the baby."

Dilly was speechless for a moment. "You tended the baby? What baby?"

"The new baby—the one they were having the shower for."

"That won't be needed here, they have a nurse to tend the baby."

"A nurse? That's a sad state of affairs."

"Nevertheless, Dunley, you are not needed."

"How are you going to get there? I would be glad to drive you."

"No thank you, a friend is picking me up."

"All right, Dilly, if you'll just tell your friend to wait a moment, I'll get my car and follow. I promise I won't go in. I'll stay out of your way."

The honking of a horn was heard out in the front "My friend is here, let me by." Fenn moved aside. Dilly opened the door and ran down the steps. Fenn followed her to a white Mercedes parked against the curb.

"Hi Mary," Dilly said, greeting her friend through the open car window.

"Hi Mary," Fenn repeated, as Dilly walked around the car to get into the front seat. "I'm Fenn, Dilly's bodyguard. May I ride in the back seat?"

"Certainly, Fenn."

"No, he can't!" contradicted Dilly, panic in her voice as she opened the door and got in the same time Fenn got in the back.

"Of course he can, Dilly, no problem."

Dilly fumed in silence as Mary conversed with her passenger in the back seat.

"My husband and I saw you last night, Fenn, but we didn't get to meet you."

"Oh oh, I guess you read the paper this morning?"

Mary laughed. "Yes, you added a bit of color, I'd say."

Mary drove to an area of the city that no longer looked like Boston, instead had the architecture and landscaping of California. It was a lovely upper-middle-class neighborhood.

After Mary parked in front of the house, the girls got out. Fenn followed.

"Where's your gift?" Fenn asked Dilly.

"Don't you know, Fenn," she said with affected disdain, "that in proper society gifts are sent ahead? It is considered socially incorrect to carry it with you."

"Oh? That sounds inconvenient and superfluous," he said as they arrived at the front door.

The hostess greeted Dilly and Mary, then stared at Fenn disapprovingly. "Is this the party crasher of last night that we read about in the paper?"

"I'm afraid it is," Dilly said, rolling her eyes.

Fenn remained on the porch after the other two walked in. Reaching out his hand to the hostess, he said, "My name is Fenn Dinkle, and yours?"

She ignored his outstretched hand and said with a touch of coolness, "I'm Meg Holland, you may come in."

"That's nice of you, ma'am, but as you see, I'm not dressed for the occasion and besides," he grinned, "I hear men are not invited."

Before Meg could close the door, a couple of young women from inside the house raised their voices in protest.

"Meg, if that is the infamous bodyguard of Dilly's, invite him in."

"I did," Meg replied holding back her irritation, "but he declined. Besides, I believe our guest of honor might prefer to have this remain an all female shower."

The two young women appeared at the door, and pushing past Meg stepped out onto the porch. They introduced themselves, and in spite of Meg, invited him to attend.

"We are also hosting this shower. We know that Shari, our guest of honor, will not mind at all," one of them assured him.

"Thank you, but I think I'll just mosey around the neighborhood, and admire the homes and landscaping."

"Well, come back in a while," the other one said, "and we'll bring you out some refreshments."

"Sounds good, thanks," Fenn said, smiling dutifully, glad to escape.

Inside, the girls approached Dilly. "Where did your aunt find that hunk?"

"What hunk?" she asked, feigning ignorance.

"You know, Dilly, your new bodyguard."

"What do you mean by hunk? I haven't heard that term in ages."

"Hunk to me," replied one, "is overall male appeal."

"To me," explained the other one, "it's totally attractive."

Dilly thought a minute. "Well, since you are the only two single girls in this group, besides myself, he's all yours."

After an hour of walking around the neighborhood, Fenn sat under a tree in the hostess' back yard. He had just leaned against the tree, closed his eyes, savoring a moment of peacefulness when he heard someone calling, "Mr. Dinkle! Mr. Dinkle!"

Jumping up, he ran around to the front yard and found Meg Holland, frowning and distraught.

"Oh, there you are," she said relieved. "Dilly said you were good with babies."

"Well, I don't know about that—but as the oldest of eight, I've had a little practice."

"Our guest of honor, Shari, is beside herself. Her nurse can't get the baby to quit crying."

"Can't the mother calm the baby?"

"Well, this is her first and she has only played with the baby. The nurse does the rest and now the nurse seems to be unable to...uh...well...we'd like to serve refreshments to everyone and I was wondering if you could give it a try."

"I will, but only if Dilly asks me."

Meg went back into the house and Fenn waited on the front porch. Presently Dilly came out.

"Since when did you need to have my personal invitation about anything, Fenn Dinkle?"

"Since now. I can't promise results, but I'll try to calm the baby if you'll tell me about your plans tonight."

"Fenn, you are a..." she paused, searching for the right word, "a blackmailer!"

"You bet," he said, grinning.

"All right," she said thoroughly irritated. "I'm going out at 8:00 P.M. One other couple is meeting at my date's apartment and we're all watching videos, so you see I'll be perfectly safe. And—as you know, you are not invited."

"Good. Sounds boring. I'll wait in the car."

The crying of the baby was louder now. "Are you coming?"

"Lead the way."

The harried young mother hovered around the frustrated nurse. "I'm Shari, the mother of the baby," she said to Fenn, speaking above the escalating cries. "I hear you're good with babies."

"I don't know how good I am, Shari, but I've had a little practice with my younger siblings."

"The baby has been fed and changed," explained the grateful nurse as she handed the baby to Fenn.

"Her name is Samantha and she's a month old," added the mother.

Fenn smiled as he took Samantha into his arms. Holding her snugly against his chest, he began walking her back and forth in the foyer, making little reassuring sounds. As the baby's cries became less frantic, Fenn began talking to her in a soothing tone. Soon, she was totally quiet, listening to Fenn's voice.

Dilly, Shari, the nurse and everyone present watched in awe.

Fenn whispered, "All of you go in and have your refreshments."

When the shower was over, Dilly and her friend, Mary, waited for Fenn to hand Samantha over to the nurse.

"How can I thank you, Mr. Dinkle?" asked Shari. "You can give the baby back to the nurse now."

"No," Fenn said firmly.

The new mother looked anxiously over at Dilly who just shrugged her shoulders and smiled, wondering herself what Fenn was up to this time. He was turning out to be unpredictable as well—an enigma.

"I'll give Samantha to *you*."

"But...but she is asleep so the nurse will take over."

"You want to know how to thank me, Shari?"

"Yes."

"Take over the full time care of Samantha and fire this nurse."

"Of all the nerve!" spluttered the nurse.

"Well," exclaimed Shari, affronted, "you certainly are not her mother, and she did very well with you."

Acting as though he hadn't heard her, he handed Shari the sleeping baby. "There is nothing to feel anxious about," he said in a fatherly tone. "You'll be a good mother, it just takes a little practice."

"Thank you for the advice, Mr. Dinkle," Shari said in a distinctly cool voice.

Coolness also emanated from Mary during the drive home. Uh oh, Fenn thought, I've stepped on her toes too. She must also use a nurse. Dilly certainly wasn't helping out either. He couldn't help wondering why *she* was so silent. Oh well, he didn't care. This high society business was getting monotonous anyway. At least he felt better having given the unwanted advice. Maybe the young mother will change her mind and care for the baby herself. It was worth a try. He leaned back, relaxed and smiled.

~~~~~~~~~~~~

During dinner, Dilly chatted with her Aunt Isadora about the shower, telling her who was there, who was expecting and so on. Fenn kept waiting for Dilly's request that he be fired for stepping into Shari's business, but it wasn't forthcoming, at the moment anyway.

Finally, Fenn, wanting to get it over with, asked, "Dilly, aren't you going to tell your aunt about my social 'incivility' today as the society editor termed it in the paper —of which she suggested you had a flamboyant disregard?" He grinned at her. She pursed her lips and lifted her brows in a wouldn't-you-like-to-know look.

Isadora raised her eyebrows. "Why yes, Dilly, by all means tell me the latest."

"It was definitely a social faux pas, Aunt Issy."

"Since when did you ever feel concerned about a social faux pas, Dilly?" her aunt said, smiling. "Tell me what happened."

"Never mind, you wouldn't fire him after hearing it anyway—in fact, you'd probably just give him another raise—so I'm not going to waste my breath."

"You tell me then, Fenn."

"Oh but Dilly tells it with such a flare," Fenn said, his eyes narrowing as he smiled. Dilly was acutely aware of the tiny laugh lines that fanned out from the corner of each eye.

"Tell me, Fenn," Isadora insisted.

"Yes ma'am." He told it as quickly and concisely as he could—then waited for a reaction.

"He left out details," commented Dilly.

Isadora, trying to understand such a condensed version, was thoughtful for a moment, then she nodded, smiling.

"You're right, Dilly, I *am* going to give him another raise."

Fenn smiled smugly as he watched Dilly.

Her eyes narrowing, Dilly spoke in an ominous tone. "You wait, Fenn Dinkle, your time is coming."

Isadora pulled out a checkbook from her pocket. "It's Saturday, Fenn. I pay salaries on Saturday." She wrote the check and handed it to him.

Fenn took it and looked at it; his eyes widened in shock. "Two thousand dollars! Wait a minute here, Isadora!" he exclaimed. "This is a lot of money for only four days. Your raises are some raises." He looked over at Dilly, who was watching him curiously. He thought a moment. "On the other hand..." he paused again, weighing it carefully. "Maybe it's not too much. Dilly's doing her darnedest to shorten my career as a bodyguard. Scratch my protests Isadora, the four days seem like four weeks anyhow. I may be out of a job soon—if Dilly has anything to do with it, and I'll have to make up for lost time."

# Chapter Fifteen

Fenn waited in his car in front of the neighbor's brownstone for Dilly's date to arrive. Expecting a long evening in the car, he brought his work and a flashlight.

Ever since holding Dilly in his arms at the dance, he found his thoughts dwelling more and more on her. But his thoughts disturbed him. Yeah, so he was attracted to her—what guy wouldn't be, he told himself. In fact, he realized the minute he saw her he was intrigued—but as soon as she opened her mouth, he had an intense urge to turn her over his knee. He felt no differently now. An attraction was all it was, and it was going to stay that way. He wasn't going to join the ranks of all the other goofy-headed males who were masochistic enough to hope they could make her fall in love with them!

A Porsche drove up at 8:00 P.M. and parked in front of Isadora's. A man in casual pants and shirt got out, walked up the steps and rang the door bell. Dilly opened the door looking very attractive in a sienna-colored shirt, white pants and a white jacket draped over her arm. No sooner had she opened the door, than she was out.

Hmn, thought Fenn, she doesn't want Isadora to meet her date. Studying the man, he noted, from where his car was parked, that he looked to be at least forty and was what most women would call hand-some. Through the years, Fenn, as an older brother, watched out for his sisters. He learned how to spot a snake in the grass, and this man struck him as definite snake in the grass material. He would know for sure when he could look him in the eye. Dilly glanced in his direction momentarily, then got into the car.

The Porsche led him downtown and ended up driving into the underground parking of a swank high rise apartment building. Fenn quickly parked in the first empty spot and followed them to the elevator, staying out of sight until it opened, then ran and got on with them.

"Hello, I'm Fenn, Dilladora's bodyguard," he said, holding out his hand to Dilly's date. The man was so startled he wasn't even aware of Fenn's outstretched hand.

"You didn't tell me you had a bodyguard!" he exclaimed, wariness and anger in his voice.

"Don't worry, Hank, he's harmless," Dilly said, giving Fenn a patronizing smile. "Aunt Isadora hired him because of a silly kidnapping scare a while back. Fenn, this is Hank Judd, a new attorney in town."

"Glad to meet you, Hank," Fenn said, studying his face carefully. The old familiar jab-in-the-gut told him that his first impression was right. The man was up to no good.

The elevator stopped at the tenth floor and Fenn got off with them. Hank Judd stiffened perceptibly when Fenn walked with them down the hall to number 1008.

Hank turned to Fenn, his eyes seething with suspicion. "And what do *you* intend to do, Mister?"

"Oh nothing, I just wanted to see you both to the door. I'll be waiting in my car down stairs—just doing my job, Hank." Fenn raised his hands, palms outward, "Just doing my job."

Hank put the key in the lock and opened the door.

"Bye, Fenn," Dilly said smiling. "Have a nice evening in the car." The door closed behind them.

What in the heck was he going to do now? he wondered. He paced the hall. The answer came when the elevator coughed up one more couple who also stopped at number 1008. They rang the bell. When the door opened, he heard Dilly's voice. "Gloria!" At least she seemed to know one of them quite well, he thought with some relief.

Fenn pushed himself inside the room with the couple, reached back, felt the door knob, found the lock and turned it to what he hoped was the unlock position. It was at that moment Hank Judd noticed him.

"What in the hell are *you* doing in here?"

"I just wanted to meet these folks before I went down stairs. Just doing my job, Hank, just doing my job." He smiled. Introducing himself, he shook each of their hands while scrutinizing their surprised and blank faces. Dilly stifled a giggle. He backed out and with a wave of his hand bid them good evening. Pulling the door shut, he stood outside, his ear against the door, listening. As he hoped, Hank didn't check the lock.

If Dilly was correct, this was the last of the guests. When twenty minutes had passed, he felt safe in surmising that there would be no one else entering apartment 1008. Now what was he going to do? He might as well forget trying to write, he couldn't keep his mind on it for worrying about Dilly. Listening at the door, he heard laughing and talking and the clink of glasses. Apparently they were having some kind of drink before the entertainment.

He didn't know what to expect from Hank Judd. Nevertheless he sat down by the door hoping other apartment dwellers on this floor would not show up and wonder what he was doing there. He planned several strategies in case something went wrong and also tried to guess what Dilly might do.

After about an hour things quieted down. They were watching a video. Hearing laughter now and then, Fenn began to wonder if he was wrong, when all of a sudden he heard a commotion. He shot to his feet. Quietly cracking the door, he peeked in and saw Dilly walk to the VCR. She angrily ejected the video, something he hadn't expected of course. She held it in her hand.

"I told you the only kind of video I watch, Hank Judd!"

"Awe come on, baby, it's just a comedy, I didn't realize you would mind a little adult humor. We're all adults here."

"Come off it, Dilly." Gloria added. "Don't pull that pure little girl stuff on us, you've been in a few escapades."

"Not the kind you're thinking of, Gloria."

"Come on, baby, put the video back in," wheedled Hank.

"I'm sorry, Hank," she said dropping the video onto the floor and stomping on it. "It seems to be broken."

"Why you little witch!" Hank lunged for her.

Fenn slipped in carefully and quickly, hiding behind the hall tree, hoping Dilly could hold her own for a few moments. Since the other couple's attention was on Hank and Dilly, he decided on a long shot. Grabbing Dilly's jacket from the hall tree, he used it to pick up a video from a pile of them on a nearby shelf. Wrapping it up, he turned toward the struggle just in time to see Dilly knock Hank Judd to the floor with a move that was almost too fast to follow. Everyone stood staring at the stunned man whose nose was bleeding.

Fenn whispered, "Come on, Dilly!"

Astounded to see him, she looked blank.

"Come on!" he ordered. She stepped quickly past Hank and they almost made it to the door.

"Wait a minute!" the other man yelled. "You're not going anywhere."

Fenn turned and saw the man's face and knew instinctively that he was the same ilk as Hank Judd. Fenn backed up as if in fear, then used a rusty but carefully timed kick, putting this miscreant out of action. They ran to the elevator which luckily had remained on their floor. It opened immediately and closed, carrying them safely to the parking lot.

Grabbing Dilly's hand, they dashed to the car. Fenn quickly unlocked the door for her and she got in. Running around, he climbed into the driver's seat, letting the video slip carefully out of Dilly's jacket onto the floor behind his seat, hoping she wouldn't notice.

"Here's your jacket," he said handing it to her.

"What? You took the time to grab my jacket?"

"Yes," he said backing up. Tires squealed as he sped out of the underground parking lot to the street.

Dilly laughed. "What's the hurry, Dunley? They're certainly in no condition to follow us."

"You mean you aren't scared?" he asked, aghast at her cavalier attitude.

"No, I've been in scrapes before."

"This kind?"

"Well, not exactly but similar," she hedged. "I might add, you did quite a number on that guy."

Fenn, seething with anger, exclaimed, "You ought to be spanked! You're old enough to know the danger in these kind of situations."

"Why—you're angry, Dunley. I didn't know you could get angry," she taunted.

Fenn's knuckles grew white as he gripped the wheel, not trusting himself to speak. Dilly fell silent as she noticed Fenn's jaw ripple in anger. She remained silent the rest of the way home.

Stopping in front of Isadora's, Fenn waited for her to get out.

"Thank you for..."

"Don't thank me, just get out."

"All right, I won't thank you." She got out, slammed the door hard and ran up the steps. Reaching into the pocket of her jacket she got her key, which was amazingly still there, and opened the door. She turned and waved.

Not acknowledging it, he drove off around to his apartment. He ran upstairs and came right back down with a clean handkerchief and a plastic bag. Picking up the video with the hanky, he slid it into the bag.

Back upstairs, he sat down, placing the hanky and bagged video on the floor beside the chair. Only then did he acknowledge how truly shaken he was by the events of the last hour. What if something had happened to Dilly—he shook his head and closed his eyes—trying to shake off the dreadful thought.

He felt that Hank Judd was into something sinister but didn't know what. When he calmed down, and was able to think more clearly, he knew what he had to do, for the moment at least.

Running down the steps and around to the front door of Sophie and Max's cottage, Fenn knocked. Max answered the door.

"Why, Fenn boy, this is a surprise. Come on in."

"Thank you, Max."

"Mr. Fenn!" exclaimed Sophie, an expression of concern on her face. "Is something wrong?"

"Don't worry, Sophie, Dilly is safe. I need to talk to Isadora but I don't want Dilly to know about it, for now anyway. Do you think you could find a way to ask Isadora to come up to my apartment?"

"I sure can, Mr. Fenn, I can think of a good excuse in case I run into that girl."

"Thank you, Sophie."

Back upstairs, Fenn paced the floor, thinking. Finally he heard a knock. He opened the door to see a very anxious Isadora.

"What is it, Fenn?"

"Come in, Isadora. Please sit down. It may not be anything at all, but I need to tell you what happened tonight."

He went over every detail of the evening, including his first feeling about Hank Judd. In recounting it, Fenn found himself becoming agitated again. Anger over Dilly's lighthearted treatment of the danger propelled him up out of his chair. He stalked the floor.

"She laughed, Isadora. She has no sense of the real danger she was in! How can we impress it upon her that even in this low crime city, there are real dangers if you allow yourself to be in certain situations? If it wasn't against the contract, Isadora, I would have followed her into the house and turned her over my knee."

Isadora's head followed Fenn as his restless stride carried him around the room. "Fenn, from what I know of you, you don't get upset easily and you rarely get angry. Am I correct?"

He stopped a moment and looked down at her. "Yes."

"Then why are you this upset?"

"Dang it, Isadora, aren't you upset?"

"I'm very upset, but she's like a daughter to me. What is she to you?"

Fenn frowned, puzzled. "Well...while I am in your employ, she's my responsibility."

"You feel responsible for her?"

"That's right."

"Is that all you feel?"

He stared at her in disbelief. "Is that all I feel? I can't believe you're asking that question. Believe me, you have no need to worry that way. She's a willful, strong-headed, stubborn and exasperating girl! No way would I want to get myself tangled up with her. If you have worries about that, Isadora, put them to rest."

"Did I say I had worries, Fenn?"

"Well...not in so many words. But—you should have worries that I'll chain her to the bedstead and throw away the key!"

Isadora smiled. "Sit down, Fenn and let's talk reasonably and calmly about tonight. What are your concerns?"

Fenn sat and exhaled heavily. "The least of my worries is that Hank Judd and his friend, who were injured by Dilly and me, will each file a law suit against the wealthy Mrs. Isadora Penbroke—and they may have grounds—unless..."

"Unless what?"

"The 'unless' brings me to my greatest concern—unless there is something of a criminal nature involved. As I mentioned, I get these hunches sometimes. Most of the time they're correct, though I do miss on a few. I have a hunch that Hank Judd and his friend are into some-thing—I don't know, maybe something as serious as drug peddling."

Isadora turned pale. "You think they are selling it here in Bostonville?"

"Whatever they're up to, they are settling here in Bostonville. Maybe they're hiding out, who knows. This is a place where the authorities would least likely look. I have a feeling that if they're into something like drugs, they aren't just your corner drug pushers. Hank Judd is too savvy and hard.

"I wish that Obadiah were here." Isadora, the confident, self-pos-sessed woman had become a frightened and vulnerable one.

Fenn got up and sat beside her on the couch. Putting his arm around her shoulders, he said in a soothing, confident tone, "It will be all right, Isadora. I have a plan."

"You do?"

"Yes," he said removing his arm. "Do you know if your police force is free of corruption?"

"As far as I know."

"Is there anyone in the force you can be fairly sure you can trust?"

"Yes."

"There are finger prints on the video. I'm hoping they are only Hank Judd's and not smudged beyond recognition. We need them taken off and sent to the FBI. Do you know someone in that department?"

"Yes, Obadiah had a close friend high up in the FBI."

"Good. Money and connections come in mighty handy sometimes, Isadora—like now. Can you take the video down in a briefcase Monday morning and get that done?"

"I can."

"My concerns may not be valid and I may end up with egg on my face, but better that than having Dilly get hurt. We need to keep that kind of thing out of Bostonville. If it turns out that something illegal is going on, Dilly needs a good scare."

"I agree whole heartedly, Fenn."

"I want her to know about it only after we find out a few things, but it's up to you, Isadora."

"Yes, we need to wait and find out and then—I hope we can give Dilly the scare of her life."

"You know what that may mean, don't you, Isadora?"

"What?"

"It's possible that Dilly won't need a bodyguard anymore."

# Chapter Sixteen

"Help!" called the beautiful princess from the high turret window of the castle. "Help!"

"I'm coming! I'm coming!" the prince yelled back as he struggled with all his might to swim the dark mote. But—no matter how strenuous his swimming strokes, no matter how hard he kicked his legs, he remained in one spot.

"Help!" That last cry seemed to unlock the spell. He began inching forward and at last—he reached the castle!

"I've made it! Open the draw bridge, princess!" yelled the prince.

"Open the draw bridge?" the princess questioned him.

"Yes, hurry, I'm sinking!"

"No," replied the princess.

"But I have come to rescue you, open the drawbridge!"

"No, I don't want to," she called back—then she laughed. The princess laughed!

Fenn woke up with a start and found himself perspiring again—and very relieved to find he wasn't drowning. Or was he? he asked himself as the real nightmare of last night came to mind. Putting his hands behind his head, he tried to go over the events of the evening before, but could not concentrate. Instead, he found himself still simmering over the witless princess of his dream. Shaking his head, trying to throw off the mood, he glanced at his watch.

"It's Sunday. My free day!" he exclaimed aloud—a chance to recuperate from the last four harrowing days and nights. Ruminating on how great this felt, he jumped out of bed and began to get ready for church.

~~~~~~~~~~~~

Arriving home after church, Fenn decided to check with Sophie concerning lunch before going up to his apartment. Walking across the veranda, something caught the corner of his eye. Turning, he saw the most enchanting sight he'd ever seen—Dilly sitting in the swing which hung from the large old tree. Ever so slightly swinging, her long all white dress, a light filmy cotton, fluttered with the tenuous breeze created by the back and forth movement. Her face pensive, her eyes staring at the ground, she looked as ethereal as an angel.

Like a magnet, he was drawn to this vision of loveliness. As he got closer, he noticed a sprig of tiny, white, bell-like flowers stuck in her hair—which, like her white dress, enhanced its lovely red hues. He stopped, trying to take it all in, wishing he had a camera to capture the picture before the spell was broken.

Slowly her head lifted; her blue eyes brightened with surprise. "Dunley!"

"Dillweed," he returned softly.

"Where have you been all dressed up?" she asked.

"To church like my mother taught me. Why are you all dressed up?"

"I've been to church like Aunt Issy and Uncle Obi taught *me*."

They smiled at each other. A rare moment, Fenn thought.

"Are you over your mad, Dunley?"

"I guess so. But I'm still mad at that princess."

"The princess?" Dilly cocked her head in surprise. "What princess?"

"The princess in my dream."

"Oh." She grinned. "Tell me about it."

"No," he said. The thoughts of telling it propelled him around. "See you later Dilly."

"Fenn, wait! You can't leave me wondering about that princess."

He smiled at her as he turned around. "Fenn? You call me Fenn when you want your curiosity satisfied?"

"Please?" she coaxed.

"This is my day off, Dilly." He smiled, swinging his arms wide. "I'm free as a bird! I don't have to do your bidding today."

"Do it then because you want to," she said patting the bench beside her, a winsome and alluring smile upon her face.

Fenn laughed. "Is that how you beguiled all those other poor bodyguards—causing their downfall?"

"How can you be so suspicious?" she asked with captivating innocence.

Fenn remained standing, smiling, but not moving any closer.

"I promise I won't beguile you," she said in a normal tone of voice.

"It's too late."

"Too late?"

"You've already beguiled me."

"I have?" she asked, her eyes wide in astonishment.

"Yeah."

"When?"

Fenn thought a moment. "I think I could figure it out if I really put my mind to it, but don't get your hopes up expecting to use it to further your campaign. I'm an expert in beguilement."

Dilly raised her eyebrows, a half smile on her face. "And how did you get to be an expert, Dunley?"

"I'll make a deal with you Dilly. I will answer your two questions after you answer my two questions—first."

"What are the questions?" she asked, suddenly wary.

"Make the deal, or no deal."

"You are so tenacious, Fenn Dinkle. All right, it's a deal."

Fenn eyed the inviting swing and then the lawn. Dressed in his Sunday suit, the lawn was out. He sat in the swing as far away from the other occupant as he could get, which, in his mind, was not far enough. The scent of her perfume floated his way. He caught his breath, again remembering when he held her in his arms. With great difficulty he tried to put it out of his mind.

Some distance away, a pair of eyes watched them—interested—curious.

"Mr. Fenn had better watch his step," stated a loud voice behind Isadora, causing her to nearly jump out of her skin.

Isadora clutched at her chest. "Sophie! Don't come up behind me like that."

"Sorry, Issy Mum. You feeling a might guilty spying on those two?"

"Don't be ridiculous, Sophie," answered Isadora a bit too quickly, then turning from the back door window she walked with purposeful steps toward the library.

Disgruntled, Sophie frowned as she watched Dilly and Fenn sitting together in the swing. She grumbled under her breath, "That girl is going to get that boy fired yet. He'd better watch his step."

She turned away and marched into the kitchen to finish preparing dinner, banging cupboard doors and pans louder than usual.

Fenn and Dilly were quiet for some time, enjoying the gentle motion of the swing and the mellow warmth of the California sun.

"Ah, a little bit of heaven here, Dilly. A respite I sorely needed. I want a swing like this on my back porch some day."

"What are your questions, Dunley?"

"Tell me about your mother."

"My mother?" she asked in surprise.

"Yes."

"Why do you want to know?"

"Just do, that's all."

Dilly thought a moment, then a wistful faraway look appeared on her face. "Did you know that my mother named me Dilladora after Isadora?" Fenn shook his head. "My mother brought fun and excitement into my life when she came to visit. It was always a whirl of activity: ballooning, scuba diving, musicals and so on. Then she would leave as suddenly as she came."

"How did you feel about her coming and going like that?"

"I just accepted it because that was all I had known. I only questioned it when I discovered that my friends had mothers who were around all the time."

"And then?" pursued Fenn as Dilly became silent.

"Then I fell into the doldrums. Uncle Obi came to my rescue and we read together and made the world come alive with literature and history. Aunt Issy joined us, suggesting we make a time line showing when all the great literature was written, along with corresponding historical events—but asked that we use the Bible dates and stories as the *core* events. The fun and excitement of the three of us learning together far surpassed the adventures with my mother. This made me feel that I was luckier than other children whose mothers were always around and it was then that Aunt Issy and Uncle Obi, in my mind, became my parents and Lilly, my mother, became my visiting relative."

Fenn, quite impressed with the story, sat there thinking for a while. "Unusual folks, your aunt and uncle."

"Yes, they are. What is your next question?"

"I'm not finished with the first. What happened to your mother?"

"I don't think she ever got over my father's death. Even though she was beautiful, she never remarried. She seemed to be running away from life all the time by tripping all over the world, mountain climbing, skydiving and finally—she crashed while piloting her own small plane."

"I'm sorry, Dilly."

"Thank you."

"Her activities must have taken a lot of money."

"She was my Uncle Obadiah's sister, so she was well off—to her detriment I'm afraid. Next question," she stated firmly, anxious to get it over with so she could ask her own.

"Why are you taking psychology classes?"

"I'm going to be a counselor."

"What kind of a counselor?"

"You said only two questions."

"A question has many parts, Dilladora, you know that. If you want me to answer you with one sentence, so be it."

"But I have answered several questions already, and my personal life is none of your business."

"The deal's off." Fenn got to his feet and started toward his apartment.

"Fenn, come back!"

He turned, walked back grinning. "All right, go on," he said sitting down.

"Ooh! Fenn Dinkle, you infuriate me."

"This is my day off, you don't have to be infuriated today."

Dilly giggled, the giggles turning to laughter.

"Am I going to have to get out a hanky?"

"No," she retorted, quickly sobering.

"I'm waiting for the answer."

"I'm going to be a youth counselor."

"Why?"

"Because I want to."

"Why?"

Dilly fumed a moment then answered. "Because they won't let me teach like I want to—and this is the next best thing I can do to work with youth."

For some reason Fenn was not surprised at this new insight into Dilly. "Who won't let you teach the way you want?"

"The school curriculum, the school boards, the state, the parents."

"You *were* a teacher?"

"Of course, how else would I teach?"

"Knowing you, I think you could probably find a way," he said, smiling. "What did you teach?"

"I graduated from Bostontown University with a degree in History. For three years I taught at a junior high school in Medford City. I finally quit after they threatened to fire me several times."

"Who are 'they'?"

"A few parents, and the school board."

Fenn was smiling. "Did you tell a few parents off?"

"How did you know?"

"I witnessed how you handled the man in the Medford Consortium building and that construction worker."

"The parents deserved it."

"So did the construction worker," Fenn said.

"You don't think the man in the Consortium building did?"

"He did, but you shouldn't have handled it that way with him."

"Why?" she asked in a defiant tone.

"Because he's a mean one, Dilly. If he ever saw you again, you'd be in danger. If you wouldn't do things like that, you wouldn't have to put up with me right now."

"Dillweed!" yelled Sophie from the back porch. "Dinner is ready."

"Now what did I do to pique Sophie today?" Dilly asked herself out loud.

~~~~~~~~~~

After dinner, Fenn and Dilly ensconced themselves in patio chairs under the veranda roof. Even the leaves of the old tree that held the swing didn't filter out enough of the now very warm California sun.

Fenn was grateful. He felt much more comfortable in a separate chair facing Dilly than next to her.

Dinner had been served in the dining room. It was the Penbroke tradition to be more formal on Sunday midday, Fenn learned. He also learned that casual dress was suitable for the main meal every day except on the Sabbath. Since no one informed him of this, Fenn was glad he hadn't changed his Sunday clothes. Max and Sophie sat at the table, also in their Sunday best. Dinner was enjoyable, but Dilly was more quiet than usual. Max asked questions about Fenn's family so he had entertained them with humorous stories about his sisters and brothers.

Removing his suit coat, Fenn folded it over the back of another patio chair, leaned toward Dilly, his arms resting upon his knees.

"It's your turn Dilly—a deal is a deal," he said, noticing her far away expression.

"What? Oh yes." A sly smile stole over her face. "The first question is, how did you get to be an expert in beguilement?"

He grinned. "You figuring on embarrassing me, Dilly?"

She didn't answer, just studied his face carefully.

"Wel-l," he drawled, "I learned by watching my three younger sisters, Emmeline, Lavinnia and Cecelia." The look of disappointment on Dilly's face made him laugh.

Dilly squinted her eyes. "Are you being totally honest with me, Fenn Dinkle?"

"Scout's honor," he said showing the Scout sign.

"You were a Boy Scout?"

"Yep."

"And an Eagle Scout no doubt."

"Yep."

"Well, so much for that. Now tell me about the princess in your dream."

"Awe, Dilly, I was hoping you would forget about that," he said, "it's just a nonsensical dream."

"A deal is a deal, Dunley."

"All right, but I want you to know I don't dream dreams like this usually, especially having one dream a continuation of the other on two consecutive nights.

"Really?" Dilly leaned forward, her eyes alight with curiosity."

Reluctantly he began by telling the first dream. Dilly was amused. As he got into the second dream, he surprised himself. Frustration and anger at the princess flared up again and Dilly's giggles didn't help; in fact, they annoyed him immensely. By the time he finished the narrative, he was thoroughly angry.

"Stupid princess," he blurted out.

Dilly laughed. Fenn frowned. There was something familiar here. It was Dilly's laughter!

"Dilladora stop it," he demanded.

Shocked at his tone of voice, she stopped. "Why?"

"Because your laughter sounds just like that...that witless princess."

"You...you mean *I* am the princess in your dream?"

He glared at her. "It appears so."

Dilladora collapsed into helpless laughter. Fenn, still glowering, automatically pulled out his hanky and waited, not amused at all. Finally her hand reached out expectantly. Fenn looked at her hand, then at the hanky, then back at her hand. His eyes narrowed. Suddenly he stood up, and shoved the hanky back into his pocket.

"Go find your own hanky—*Princess Dillweed*!" With long quick steps, he made a beeline for his apartment, leaving a surprised Dilly staring after him, mouth open, tears rolling down her cheeks and nose running.

This mutinous outburst served only to heighten her amusement. She got up and ran into the kitchen to find her own hanky—which, ignoring Sophie's indignant protests, turned out to be the first handy dish towel.

# *Chapter Seventeen*

Monday morning at 11:50 A.M., Fenn watched as the last passenger got on the bus. No Dilly.

Since he was not welcome in the child psychology class, he had decided to wait for Dilly at the bus stop. Sitting on the floor outside the classroom last time hadn't worked out well at all. Besides, a bench was more comfortable.

Fenn was unconcerned when Dilly didn't show up. He casually walked back to the cafeteria to look around in case she stopped in for something to eat before going home.

Twenty minutes later after eating a sandwich, Fenn went to the phone to call Sophie, sure that Dilly had gotten a ride home again.

"Penbroke residence," stated Sophie.

"Sophie, this is Fenn. Is Dilly there yet?"

"Why no, she's not expected home 'till 4:30 or 5:00."

"She isn't?" he gulped. "Can you tell me where she went?"

"You know I can't, Mr. Fenn. And you know as well as I do that I shouldn't have told you that much."

"Thanks, Sophie, I appreciate it." Fenn hung up the phone, concerned.

The contract gave him only an hour-and-a-half leeway after losing track of Dilly. He was in a real pickle this time. Sitting at one of the tables, he tried to think about it calmly. At the moment it appeared there was no way to find out where in the blazes that girl had gone.

Five minutes later, an idea came to him. It was a long shot but it was all he had. He dashed out of the cafeteria. Dodging students, he ran to Dr. Bonham's classroom. It was empty. Stopping a young man in the hall, he asked where the administration building was and found, to his relief, that it was the very next building. He arrived there quickly. Stopping at the office, he asked the whereabouts of Dr. Bonham's office. Learning that it was on the first floor of this very building, he thanked the young woman and ran. Finding the door open, he saw Dr. Bonham standing at his desk putting papers into a briefcase.

"Dr. Bonham?" gasped Fenn, out of breath.

"Yes?"

"Do you...uh, could I have a moment of your time?"

"A moment only, I have an appointment with my wife this after-noon."

"Thank you. My name is Fenn Dinkle. I am Dilladora Dobson's bodyguard."

"Yes," he said "I remember you. Have a seat."

"I don't have time to sit, Dr. Bonham. I've lost Dilly, I mean, she's lost me. Deliberately. I've got to find her soon or I'll set the record by being the first of her bodyguards to be fired after only five days."

Dr. Bonham chuckled. "An interesting family—an amusing situation."

"Do you have any idea where she is right now?"

"As a matter of fact, I do. She's gone to Medford City Social Services to start her tenure as an assistant counselor. Today is her first day. She'll be going there Monday, Wednesday and Friday afternoons."

Relief written all over Fenn's face, he asked, "Do you know the address?"

"No, but I can look it up for you," he said, pulling out a phone book. Finding it, he wrote the address down on a slip of paper and handed it to Fenn.

"I can't thank you enough, Dr. Bonham." The smile on Fenn's face soon disappeared as he glanced at his watch. "I've just missed the Medford City bus!"

"Don't you have a car, son?"

"I do, Dr. Bonham. Thank you. I'll catch the other bus and go get it."

"Let me drop you off at your place, Mr. Dinkle. I'll still have time to make my appointment."

"I would appreciate that very much."

Once in the car, Fenn relaxed. "I want to tell you, Dr. Bonham, I find your lectures very enlightening. I take notes and have received ideas from them for my columns."

"You have a newspaper column, Mr. Dinkle?"

"Please call me Fenn. Yes, I have a column that the papers use whenever they don't know what else to put there."

"Why, I believe I've read your column several times. I knew your name was familiar when I first heard it—but never associated it with a bodyguard. They don't seem to go together, somehow." He smiled. "But I remember enjoying the humor in them."

"Thank you, sir, that means a lot to me coming from you."

Fenn noticed that Dr. Bonham didn't need instructions on how to get to Beacon Ave. and wondered if he had given Dilly a ride home now and then.

"How long did you say you've been Dilly's bodyguard, Fenn?"

"Five days."

Dr. Bonham chuckled. "Dilladora is quite a girl—but foolhardy. She complains to me about the nuisance of bodyguards, but refuses to change her ways."

"I know. And if I don't find her soon, *I* will no longer be her bodyguard and..." Fenn paused for such a long time, Dr. Bonham looked over at him, finding him in deep thought. "You know, Dr. Bonham," he said slowly, "I don't think I trust any other bodyguard to look after her."

"Oh?" Dr. Bonham raised his eyebrows and smiled. "Well, from what I observe, Fenn, Dilladora finds you more of a challenge than all the others put together. And she does love a good challenge."

"So I gather," remarked Fenn gloomily.

"You should have seen her fight to keep her place as a teacher at Medford Junior High."

"Tell me about it."

Dr. Bonham related the story of how Dilly verbally backed the school board and several irate parents into a corner with her natural wisdom. And when that didn't work, she had, several meetings later, taken the school board to task over how and what the youth should be taught—and how the parents should be helping their children.

"Several of the parents with money and power had enough clout to influence the school board. So at this point, Dilly quit before the inevitable happened."

"Her students were upset and they picketed the school board and the residences, some of which were their own parents. The principal told me that Dilly had brought around some students who were failing and several who were drop outs. It's a darn shame."

Fenn was impressed with this new insight into Dilly.

"It sounds like you're a good friend to Dilly, Dr. Bonham."

"She's taken quite a few classes from me and I've become quite attached to her. She's a remarkable girl and equally remarkable as a student. Since her Uncle Obadiah died, she has come to me often for advice."

"Has she taken it?"

"As a matter of fact, in most cases, yes."

"Could you advise her not to put herself in danger anymore?"

Dr. Bonham laughed. "I've tried, but that is where she didn't heed my advice. I believe she has an agenda, Fenn."

"So I gathered," he said again, still feeling gloomy.

As they approached the Penbroke residence, Fenn directed him to the apartment around back. When the car stopped, Fenn shook Dr. Bonham's hand affectionately.

"Thank you, sir, I appreciate this ride immensely." He stepped out of the car. "By the way," he said, sticking his head back in, "could you keep this under wraps?"

"I intend to, Fenn," Dr. Bonham answered firmly.

As Fenn fitted his long legs into his own car, he smiled, the gloom suddenly gone. He now had an ally other than Sophie.

# Chapter Eighteen

Fenn stepped into the large waiting room of the Medford City Social Services building. He sucked in his breath. The sight of waiting humanity in the stark decor of the room would challenge the bravest of souls, he mused. He found an empty seat and looked around. Gray painted walls and gray tiled floor contrasted jarringly with the drab gold plastic chairs. The walls were bare, with the exception of posted instructions for would-be recipients of county services.

Fenn studied the faces of those in his view. There were several women whose countenances had every appearance of depression. On the other side of the room his eyes slid past an angry looking man to focus instead on three mothers. Each mother was sitting next to a teenager who had all the earmarks of rebelliousness. The expression on the face of each woman seemed to be one of hopelessness. Interspersed throughout the room, several couples sat together though their body language spoke of bitter estrangement.

This isn't for Dilly! She loves life too much. These people don't appear to see any good in life. Could Dilly infect them with her optimism and zest for life, or would they eventually drag her down? Fenn pulled himself up short. This was none of his concern. He was hired only to protect Dilly from physical harm and that he'd done—so far.

Slipping the note pad from his pocket he began to work, realizing that this room, its' decor and its content, was a fertile field of ideas for the columns. He glanced up now and then to study the occupants and to see who exited the inner rooms. Two hours passed before Dilly emerged. She said something to the receptionist, then walked right past his chair, not seeing him.

He got up and followed her out, allowing her to stay a short distance ahead, enjoying the view. Her glorious red hair bounced up and down on the collar of her ivory blouse. A straight, ivory knee-length skirt showed off her nicely shaped legs, as well as the rust-colored heels. He noted admiringly that the same color of belt hugged her slim waist. All quite professional looking—with the exception of the perpetual back pack hanging from her shoulder.

He should have known something was up this morning when he saw her dressed like this. He'd never seen her in heels, not even on Sunday. Dilly was into 'comfortable'.

People from all walks of life milled up and down the sidewalk, including a group of unsavory looking teenage boys. They ogled at Dilly as they passed. All of a sudden, two of them stopped, grinning from ear to ear. The rest of the group followed suit. Fenn automatically clenched his fists and waited. He gaped in surprise. Dilly smiled with joy at seeing them, hugging each, one after the other. Fenn relaxed his fists and let out a breath, figuring that these boys must be two of her previous students.

Fenn stood there watching—marveling. This girl touched people's lives: Dr. Bonham, Joe, the bus driver, Bernie, the photographer, these boys—and, he had to admit, his own. He smiled as he thought of a few other lives she had touched—not so positively, but who would never forget her message.

When the visit was over, Dilly ran on toward the bus stop. She reached it just as a bus drove off.

Fenn walked up to her. "Need a taxi, Miss?"

Gazing at him with disbelief, she managed to whisper, "Dunley?"

"Dillweed," he responded softly, strangely sounding like an endearment.

"What are you doing here?" she asked, her voice rising. "How...how did you know where to find me?"

"That is privileged information."

She put her hands on her hips, her eyes emitting sparks. "It was Sophie wasn't it?"

"I tried to pull it out of Sophie but her lips were as tight as the lids on my mother's bottled jam."

"Sometimes I wonder if you have radar. I can't lose you, Fenn Dinkle, no matter what I do. Ooh!" she stamped her foot. "You stick to me like...like Uncle Obi's old fashioned fly paper!"

"That's what I'm being paid for." He grinned, contemplating her simile. "Was that the Bostonville bus that just drove off?"

"Yes."

"I have my car. May I give you a ride?"

She was silent.

"All right, suit yourself. If you want to pay a taxi fare that's fine with me. See you at dinner." He turned and walked nonchalantly toward the parking lot.

"Wait!"

Fenn turned around.

"I...I forgot to bring money. I would like a ride—thank you."

"You're welcome."

Dilly was pensive on the way home.

"How was the first day of counseling?"

"The youth the counselor and I worked with today—didn't want to be there. They didn't want help."

"In my book, Dilly, counseling is not for you."

Dilly's red-haired temperament flared. "You know what, Fenn Dinkle, I'm getting extremely tired of 'your book.'"

"So what else is new?"

Charged silence pervaded the car the rest of the way home. Fenn dropped Dilly off at the front, then drove around back.

Dilly opened the front door and found a stern looking Aunt Isadora waiting for her in the foyer.

"Aunt Issy, what's wrong?"

"I want to talk to you and Fenn in the library after you take your books upstairs."

"All right, I'll be right back."

Isadora retired to the library and called Fenn, then paced the floor while she waited. Dilly came in first.

"What is it, Aunt Issy?"

"I'll tell you as soon as Fenn arrives."

Fenn walked into the library, and was greeted by two concerned faces.

"Both of you please be seated," Isadora said. She handed Fenn an envelope. "Read this then pass it over to Dilly."

As Fenn opened it and read through the several pages of the legal letter, his face registered no surprise. He glanced at Isadora then handed the papers to Dilly.

It took a few moments for Dilly to understand the document, then her face paled. "Why, Aunt Issy, Hank Judd and his friend are suing you for twenty million dollars!"

"That's right, Dilladora."

"There is no way we injured those men seriously enough to warrant this suit."

"You may be right. They may be a couple of opportunists, but nevertheless, Dilladora, if you'd been more discerning about whom you go out with, this would not have happened."

Dilly was silent, distraught.

"Well, Dilladora?"

"Gloria Bradford uh...well she introduced me to those men and I assumed they were all right since she knew them."

"Since when did you ever rely on others to do your thinking?"

"You're right, Aunt Issy. I knew better than to go out with Hank Judd. I'm sorry. What are we going to do?"

"I don't know. I'll have to call my lawyer."

Sophie suddenly appeared at the library door and stated with the authority of a drill sergeant, "Dinner is on, and if you don't come now, I'll throw it to the pigs."

Dinner would have been a silent ordeal if it weren't for Max's humorous quips that made them all smile. After dinner, Dilly immediately disappeared into her room, not giving Sophie and Max her usual help in the kitchen.

Isadora whispered to Fenn after Dilly left. "I'll be up to your quarters soon. I need to talk to you."

Fenn paced the floor in his apartment, anxious to hear what Isadora had to say. He also found himself feeling badly for Dilly. Surprised that he didn't like to see her troubled, he reminded himself how eagerly he'd waited for this moment.

He heard a knock and immediately opened the door. "Isadora, come in and have a seat. Those two degenerates didn't waste any time did they?"

Isadora sat on the couch. "They certainly didn't, but I did as you said, Fenn, and took the video down to my friend, Lt. John Billings, at the police station. He arranged for the finger prints to be taken off, then immediately faxed them to my friend in the FBI. It wasn't long before

Lt. Billings received a phone call telling him that the prints matched those of a big drug dealer they have been trying to apprehend in several states."

"Wow! As I said, it pays to have connections, Isadora. This means that all along they intended to settle. No way would they want the publicity that a lawsuit would bring."

"Exactly. I'm meeting with my lawyer tomorrow. My FBI friend said to go through the motions as if I believed they were going to sue, so they won't get suspicious. He said they would be apprehending them soon and not to worry."

"That's a relief, Isadora. Are you going to tell Dilly?"

"Not yet. I want her to be scared and penitent for a while longer. Then when she hears how dangerous these men really are, maybe she'll straighten up."

# Chapter Nineteen

Tuesday afternoon, Fenn waited in the hall for Dilly's modeling session to end, making good use of the time working on his columns. So far, the day had been benign, Dilly reverting to type, totally ignored him.

Sensing that the session was about over, he glanced at his watch. It was 4:38. Dilly would be walking out any moment now. Quickly putting his notebook and pen away, he stepped into the large busy room and looked around. He didn't see her anywhere—no clothes were flying over the screen of the makeshift dressing area. He stepped over to Mavis.

"Do you know where Dilly is, Mavis?"

"She left several minutes ago with three other girls."

"I saw four girls walk by me and Dilly wasn't one of them." He heard two girls giggle.

"What's up, Mavis?"

Mavis leaned over and whispered, "Dilly borrowed a blonde wig."

"She did? Thanks, Mavis!" He turned and ran out of the room and on out of the building. Running across the street, he saw the last passenger getting on the bus. He accelerated his speed down the side walk.

Joe, looked into his left mirror, noting the lane was clear to pull out. He glanced out of the right view mirror looking for late passengers, grateful that Dilly was already safely aboard. Out of habit, he pulled out and began driving slowly when he saw a tall blond-headed young man running alongside the bus, waving frantically. Recognizing him, he pulled the bus over, stopped and opened the doors.

"Don't tell me it's contagious, Fenn," chided Joe, grinning.

"I hope not," Fenn gasped. Hearing laughter come from a seat midway down, he turned. It was Dilly, thoroughly enjoying the whole episode. He glared at her. Since the seat next to her was taken, he walked past and sat in the seat behind.

Dilly turned around and smiled sweetly. "Don't you know that it's very dangerous to run alongside the bus, Dunley?"

He gave her a sardonic smile, "I'll try to remember that, Dillweed." After a few moments he leaned up and whispered in her ear, "Where's the blonde wig?"

She turned around to him, shocked. "Who told you about that?"

"Privileged information, Miss Dobson."

"I can't believe it, Fenn Dinkle," she hissed. "You collect allies everywhere you go."

"They are really your allies, Dilly. Everyone wants you to quit acting so recklessly."

Abruptly, Dilly turned away from him. Fenn fervently hoped she was remembering the impending lawsuit—and what caused it.

The bus had gone only a couple of blocks when it stopped. The passenger next to Dilly disembarked. Another one got on, a striking looking man around forty years of age, impeccably groomed in a finely tailored suit and carrying a Moroccan leather briefcase. When looking for a seat, he noticed Dilly. Smiling, he took the vacant seat next to her.

He was good, thought Fenn, as he watched the man work. He ignored Dilly for a few moments, then made a casual remark, flashing a charismatic smile. Surely, Dilly wasn't falling for the act—or was she doing this to annoy him? It looked to him as though she was putting on an excessive amount of charm—laughing, talking and listening intently to everything he said. Finally, the man, who was on the aisle seat, casually put his left arm up over the seat and leaned toward Dilly ever so slightly. The wedding band which Fenn had noticed when he got on the bus, was conveniently missing. He heard him make a date for dinner the following evening. Dilly accepted—a bit too readily, he thought. Certain now, Fenn knew it was for *his* benefit. He had no use for the man, but was furious at Dilly! They were nearing the outskirts of Medford City when he heard the man say, "I get off in a couple of blocks."

Fenn poked the man's shoulder. "Excuse me, sir, but I happen to be acting as this young woman's brother." The man was startled, and Dilly, a defiant tilt to her head, darted him an I-dare-you-to-meddle-this-time look.

"What?"

"...this young woman's brother. Do you have any white hankies, sir?"

He heard Dilly gasp, and saw her eyes widen with alarm.

"White hankies? What in the hell is this?"

"Don't pay any attention to him, Mr. Ashton," Dilly blurted out.

"No, I want to hear this," the man said in a low voice bristling with irritation.

"You see sir, this young woman has these attacks—when her nose runs profusely and—" he shrugged his shoulders and shook his head in innocent dismay, "she never remembers to carry a hanky." The impeccably dressed man looked a little sick and Fenn continued. "You'll need to carry several white hankies. She has this fetish...she doesn't wipe her nose on anything—but *white hankies*."

The man, Mr. Ashton, if indeed that was his name, leaned away from Dilly as if she were suddenly repulsive to him, his expression reflecting it. "Is this true?"

"Well not exactly—they aren't attacks," she blustered. "My nose only runs when..."

"Never mind the unsavory details, this is my stop. It was nice to meet you." He got up quickly and walked hastily to the door, not glancing back. Fenn could see that the gentleman, if one could call him that, did not intend to keep the dinner date.

"This time—you have gone—*too* far, Fenn Dinkle," Dilly said in an ominous whisper—and somehow, Fenn knew he had.

Getting up, he sat in the empty seat next to her. "But," he whispered, "the man was married."

"He was not. He was not wearing a wedding band."

"He took it off."

"That's absurd! I don't want to talk about it any further and—I don't want to hear another word from you."

The fifteen minute ride to Bostonville was miserable for Fenn. He felt like a total heel for humiliating Dilly. Besides that, something oppressive was nagging at him—and he didn't know what.

Upon arriving at his apartment, instead of going up, he ran over to the kitchen. "Good evening, Sophie," he said as he walked in.

"Oh, Mr. Fenn," she said smiling. "Good evening."

"Would you please convey to Isadora that I won't be dining with them tonight, I have something important to do?"

"I will, Mr. Fenn. Is there something wrong?" she asked, noticing the serious face of the usually smiling young man.

"Dilly is safe, Sophie," was his noncommittal reply.

"I'll save you a plate, Mr. Fenn."

"Thank you, Sophie." He bent down, kissed her on the cheek and walked out.

Up in his apartment, Fenn paced the floor. Something was bothering him deep down on the gut level, and for the life of him he couldn't figure it out. He reviewed the six days he'd guarded Dilly, and gotten nowhere—except for one thing. Something Dr. Bonham said came to mind. In fact, it kept coming back; "Dilly finds you a challenge." Somehow this had to be part of the answer.

An hour later he *knew* the answer. He realized what was bothering him, and though very reluctant—he also knew what he had to do.

# Chapter Twenty

Wednesday morning at 6:30 Fenn walked into the library and found Isadora all dressed and coiffured, waiting for him.

"Good morning, Isadora. Thank you for meeting with me. And I might add, you look very nice so early in the morning."

"Thank you, Fenn," she said, pleased. "I believe in getting ready for the day early. We missed you last night at dinner. what is it you want to talk to me about?"

"First, he said, lowering his voice, I want to hear the latest on our would-be-litigators."

Isadora closed the doors to the room. "Please have a seat, Fenn." When both were seated, Isadora began, "I met with my attorney yesterday. He agreed to go along with the pretense until they are arrested. He is sending a letter today to their attorney requesting a detailed injury report by a mutually agreed upon physician."

"Good. Let me know the minute they are arrested, Isadora."

"I certainly will. If it hadn't been for you, Fenn, we would have had to deal with those two criminals."

"Well—I guess that brings me to the reason I requested our discussion this morning." He paused as if reluctant to go on, then blurted out, "I have to quit as of this morning."

Isadora, completely taken back, studied him a moment, then quietly asked, "Why, Fenn?"

"You'll agree that it's best that I quit when you hear what I have to say."

He stood up and began pacing the floor. Isadora waited patiently. Finally he stopped in front of her.

"I'm not good for Dilly and I haven't been from the beginning."

"But, Fenn," protested Isadora, "you have done an excellent job."

"I know I've done my best, Isadora, but it has backfired."

"What do you mean?"

"First, tell me, Isadora, did you know all the things that happened with all the nine other bodyguards?"

"Why...yes, I eventually found out."

"Now that I'm quitting, I want you to hear what's happened to me and Dilly during the past six days. You already know much of it, but not all. After I'm through, I would appreciate it if you would compare my experiences with all the others. I'll try to be brief."

Don't be too brief, Fenn. Pretend you're writing one of your columns and make it live." She smiled.

"You find that I make my columns live?"

"I do."

"Thank you," he said, beaming, "I can't think of anyone whose opinion I respect more—unless it's—Dilly."

He paced the floor again, thinking, then sat down across from her.

"As I said, Isadora, you already know some details because of your interminable questions at dinner—but here goes."

Finding Isadora a very good audience, he told it more colorfully as he got into it.

Isadora realized that Fenn had another talent—that of telling a good story. In spite of Dilly's actions which gave her cause for concern, she found herself entertained all the way through—even with the last episode yesterday when Fenn humiliated Dilly on the bus.

"Well, there you are, Isadora—the six months that happened in six days. What I want to ask you is—did any of these kinds of things happen with any of the other bodyguards?"

Isadora laughed. "No."

"How in the heck did they get themselves fired, then?"

Dilly just put up with them until she got tired enough of having them around.

Several she managed to lose longer than the specified time. Others she flirted with until they succumbed to her charms, then immediately she pulled the rug out from under them."

"She certainly has tried to lose me, but she's never flirted with me. Why do you suppose that is?"

"Would you want her to, Fenn?"

Fenn quickly stood up and resumed his pacing, "I can't answer that Isadora. All I know is, what you've told me about the other poor clowns just cements my resolve to quit."

"Why?"

He sat down again. "Dr. Bonham made a remark to me that set this whole thing off. He said, 'Dilly finds you a challenge.' Do you think he's correct, Isadora?"

She laughed. "From the moment she saw you, then when you opened your mouth, you challenged her further."

He shot to his feet. "You see, Isadora, that's it! I'm convinced that Dilladora has done things she wouldn't have, just because I represent a challenge to her and—to get my goat. She has been very upset over the law suit and concerned for you, so I know she wouldn't have accepted a dinner date with that slick Don Juan on the bus yesterday if it weren't for me." He sat down feeling spent.

Isadora studied him for some time. "I believe you're right, Fenn. I appreciate you caring for Dilly's safety—enough to forgo the salary. But—please do this much for me. Give it some more thought, don't pack up and leave just yet. Take a vacation for a few days, then come back and talk to me."

Fenn mulled this over. "All right, I'll do that. I'll go visit my folks for a couple of days—but I won't change my mind, Isadora."

"Fair enough—now let's go get some breakfast."

As they walked toward the closed doors, they opened suddenly and there stood Dilly.

"Dunley!"

"Dillweed," he said, feeling much more relaxed now. "You look mighty delectable in that sea-green blouse and skirt."

She flushed. "Still into flattery, Dunley?"

"Nope, just compliments." He smiled. "See you later, I'm starved. He walked purposefully toward the dining room where Sophie was serving a wonderful breakfast buffet.

"Well, Aunt Issy, why have you been closeted in the library with that...that rude, irritating, insensitive, opinionated would-be body-guard?"

"Let's go eat breakfast, Dilly."

"I need to talk to you."

"All right," she acquiesced, walking back to the sofa and sitting down. "Tell me, what's on your mind?"

Dilly closed the library doors and walked over to her Aunt.

"I want you to fire Fenn Dinkle."

"Why?"

"Because he sticks to me like glue. No matter how I try to ditch him, he magically shows up—grinning that silly grin of his!"

"Don't be ridiculous, Dilladora, we've talked about this before. You know you're not supposed to try to ditch him. How can he guard you, if you ditch him?"

"I don't need guarding any more, Aunt Issy," she said, sitting down. "I'm going to be more careful from now on. I feel terrible about the lawsuit."

"Careful? How can I believe you, Dilladora, when only yesterday on the bus, you accepted a dinner date with a total stranger? And a stranger who happens to be a *married man*."

Dilly was aghast. "He told you about that?"

"Yes."

"Why that low down squealer! That does it, Aunt Isadora." She stood up, totally incensed. "I'm moving out."

"You won't have to move out, Dilladora, unless you want to. Fenn has quit as of 6:30 this morning."

Dilly stared down at her aunt, a whole series of contradictory emotions playing themselves out upon her face.

"He...he's...quit?"

"Yes, Dilladora, he has quit."

"But...but he can't!"

"But," Isadora said calmly, "he can—he has."

Dilly was shaking her head like a boxer who had suffered a blow, leaving him totally confused.

"I...can't believe it. He's given up your lucrative salary, just...just like that?"

"Yes, Dilladora."

She looked at her aunt in disbelief. "He has really quit?"

"*Yes,* Dilladora."

"Ooh! That infuriating louse. I wanted him to get *fired*."

"So I gathered."

Without another word, Dilly whirled around. Striding over to the doors, her back ramrod-straight, her head held rigidly high, she was the classic picture of righteous indignation. She opened the doors vigorously, causing them to bang against the bookcases, and ran upstairs.

Isadora stared after her, wondering. Moments later, she came down with the backpack on her shoulder.

"I've been waiting for you to go to breakfast with me, Dilly. Aren't you going to eat?" her aunt asked.

"No, I am not. I refuse to eat breakfast in the same room as Fenn Dinkle."

# Chapter Twenty-One

The vehemence of her feelings sustained Dilly for some time, but the strength of it began to dissipate in the middle of the child psychology class, sapping her usual zest. She sighed, feeling unbearably bored with Mrs. Resnick's lecture.

The class finally ended, and as she stepped into the hall and walked a few paces, a voice behind her sniped, "What happened to your bodyguard, Dilladora? I didn't see him in Dr. Bonham's class today, did the poor lunk get himself fired?"

Dilly slowly turned around. Dora May Justin was smiling smugly, dressed as usual, in a short uncomfortable looking skirt.

"Your curiosity may kill you, Dora May, it does most cats," replied Dilly.

"Clever, Dilladora. Well, I owe Dunley Fennimore Dinkle one, so he'd better watch out."

"Why, because of the spider?"

"Yes! It could have been a black widow for all he knew."

"Why do you suppose he did that, Dora May?" Dilly asked, trying to fake knowledge of what happened.

"I really don't know," Dora May answered, wide eyed and innocent.

Her friend and accomplice giggled. "He must have overheard us planning to...Oww, Dora May! That hurt." The miffed friend nursed her ribs, and promptly tattled. "Dora May suggested that we get on each side of the door and trip you with a heavy string that she had in her purse."

Dora May flounced off, furious with her friend.

~~~~~~~~~~

Dilly nibbled a sandwich in the cafeteria, thinking about Fenn saving her from being tripped. She pictured him handing Dora May a pencil with a spider on it. Smiling, she remembered the commotion—the screaming—wishing she'd paid more attention. On the bus to Medford City, her spirits sagged as she thought of the counseling session ahead. This brought to mind what Fenn had said about counseling not being right for her. She tried to shake off the thought. Her innate stubbornness soon came to the rescue. "He's wrong. I'll show him," she whispered to herself, straightening her shoulders. As the minutes ticked by, however, they began to slump—Fenn Dinkle wouldn't be around for her to show him anything.

It was muggy, hot and cloudy as Isadora and Dilly sat down to dinner on the veranda. Soon the rain started. Sophie slammed a plate down in front of Dilly.

"Sophie, it wasn't my idea for Fenn Dinkle to quit."

"Humph!" replied Sophie.

"Tell her it wasn't my idea, Aunt Issy."

"It wasn't her idea, Sophie," Isadora repeated obediently.

"Humph!" replied Sophie.

"I'm a villain in my own household," grumbled Dilly, glancing at Sophie, who turned and walked into the kitchen.

"I'm glad it's raining, we needed it," remarked Isadora. "How was your day, Dilly?"

"Fine. Has Fenn packed up and left?"

"No, I suggested that he take several days off before he did so, and then come and talk to me about it. He assured me, however, that he would not change his mind."

"Where did he go?"

"Why do you want to know, Dilly?"

"Oh, I don't know, just curious."

"He went to see his family."

"He did?" her eyes brightened. "You know, he asked me one time to go with him to meet them."

"How nice," remarked Isadora. "Why didn't you go?"

"I didn't want to," she replied flippantly.

They ate in silence for a while, then Dilly asked, "Why did Fenn quit?"

"Why do *you* think he quit?"

"I have no idea, Aunt Issy, it was a cushy job if you ask me."

"If that were the case, why would he quit?"

"That's what I'm wondering. Surely he told you, Aunt Issy."

"He did."

"Then tell me."

"Why do you want to know, Dilly? Just be glad you're rid of him."

"Aunt Issy," she replied, exasperated "you know me, I'm the one who invented curiosity."

"He said he wasn't good for you—that you found it a challenge to outwit him and you did things that were not wise more often than you would have done ordinarily—just to annoy him."

Dilly's mouth dropped open and her eyes widened, then she said with an attempt at levity, "Well, that was quite astute of Dunley."

"So it's true, Dilly?"

Her smile of triumph touched only her lips. "Yes. I knew I could get rid of him some way."

"Don't pat yourself on the back too hard, Dilladora."

# Chapter Twenty-Two

The four-hour drive home Wednesday morning, gave Fenn a lot of time to think. His mind kept wandering back to Dilly, wondering what she was doing, hoping now that he wasn't around she would behave herself.

Myriad thoughts and emotions came and went as he tried to sort out his feelings. One emotion was missing—relief. He should have felt totally relieved that he didn't have to chase that foolish girl around, while at the same time trying to outwit and out think her. But for some reason, he wasn't. Probably, he reasoned, it was because he was still carrying the responsibility of her around with him. He'd soon take care of that.

~~~~~~~~~~~~

Thursday afternoon, Bernard Dumas complained. "Dilladora, what's the matter with you? Where is your usual sparkle?"

"I guess I'm just tired, Bernie."

"Tired? That has never affected your modeling before. There is no place for 'tired' in this business. Shape up girl, my time is valuable."

"I know, Bernie, I'll try to do better."

"Try? That's not enough, Dilladora. Do better."

After a few more shots, Bernie called it quits. "See you next Tuesday Dilly. Feel better—or else."

Dilly boarded the bus right on time.

"What's up Dilly?" a surprised Joe asked, smiling.

"Oh hi, Joe. My session was over early," she said sitting near him.

"Where's Fenn?"

"Fenn?"

"Yes, you know, your bodyguard."

"He quit."

"He did? Well that's a switch, Dilladora."

"Quite a switch," she muttered, "and quite a relief not to have someone following me everywhere I go."

"I can imagine. But he was a nice fellow, I liked him."

"So what's new—so did everyone else it seems."

"Did you like him, Dilladora?"

"He was totally irritating, Joe."

"You didn't answer my question."

"I never thought about it."

Joe quit asking questions and concentrated on his driving while Dilly concentrated on those who got on the bus. Finally, as she hoped, her would-be date got on looking a little nervous. Scrutinizing the passengers, not noticing Dilly at the front behind the driver, he looked relieved. Walking to the rear of the bus, he sat down.

Dilly got up and walked back to where he was sitting and fortunately found there was a seat beside him next to the window.

"Hello, Mr. Ashton."

Startled to see her, he quickly put his left hand into his pocket. "Oh hello, Miss Dobson. Uh...nice to see you."

"May I sit by you?" she asked, an eager smile plastered on her face.

"Oh...oh of course." He moved to the seat by the window, allowing her the seat on the aisle.

"Thank you."

"How...how are you?"

"I'm fine, Mr. Ashton, and feeling quite excited about our date tonight. What time will you pick me up?"

"Well, uh, you see something has come up. I'm afraid I'll have to break the date."

"Oh no!" she gasped as she put her hand over her nose. "I'm having one of those attacks. Do you have a white hanky?"

Horrified, the man frantically searched both pockets, found a tissue and gingerly handed it to her, revealing a wedding band on his left finger.

"I can't wipe my nose on a tissue!" she yelled under her hand. "I need a *white hanky*."

"I'm sorry, Miss Dobson," he said as he stood up, his face as red as a beet. "I can't help you."

As he tried to step over her to reach the aisle, Dilly cried out loudly, "Oh no, my nose is running. Help! I need a white hanky!"

Ashton tried to scramble away again. He had managed to get one foot into the aisle, when Dilly tripped him, causing him to stumble and fall against a hefty woman across the aisle. The surprised woman grunted angrily and shoved him back across to Dilly. Stumbling backwards, the momentum carried him across Dilly's lap to end up unceremoniously dumped, his head and back on the floor in front of his recently vacated seat—feet waving wildly in the air.

Joe looked into the mirror when he heard the commotion and could guess who was the cause.

"Help!" Dilly yelled. "My nose is streaming, I need a white hanky!"

"Shut up, will you?" Ashton hissed as he tried to extricate himself from the narrow space.

"How dare you tell me to shut up when I'm in distress," she said loudly as if she were about to cry, her hand still covering her nose and mouth.

The man grunted and groaned as he got to his feet. Dilly also stood up.

"Get out of my way!" he ordered.

"No, you get out of mine," she wailed.

He shoved her down and attempted to step over her. Again Dilly stuck out her foot and the unfortunate Mr., Ashton once more found himself across the aisle in the lap of the hefty woman. "Why you weasel," she bellowed, "can't you stay off me?"

"Oh, please," he whimpered "don't shove me back, I..I have to get away."

The woman lifted him up onto his feet and gave him a push down the aisle. The impeccable man was no longer so. Thoroughly disheveled and breathless, he reached backward, grabbing his briefcase from the floor where it had fallen, and began to weave unsteadily toward the front of the bus. Begging the driver to let him off at the next corner, he cast nervous glances back at the dreadful and appalling scene still going on.

Joe, shocked at the change in the man's appearance, checked the racket still emanating from the back of the bus. His glance in the rear-view mirror revealed what he suspected. It was still coming from Dilladora. Recognizing that one was connected to the other, he chuckled.

Like spectators watching a ping-pong match, the passenger's heads were swinging back and forth from the quivering and hapless man at the front to the wailing girl in the rear.

As the bus stopped at the corner, Dilly, still standing, seeing that Ashton was about to disembark, raised her voice to a pitch hitherto unreached. Ashton glanced back in panic just as he took the first step down, missing it, stumbling, and landing on his face in the curbside grass. Gathering what was left of his tattered dignity, he hobbled off down the sidewalk.

Dilly giggled as she watched. Several confused looking men in Dilly's vicinity, anxious to help the damsel in distress, had retrieved white hankies from their pockets—only to find out—the damsel was *not* in distress.

~~~~~~~~~~~

Thursday evening, all the Dinkle family, with the exception of Fred and Chester who were away at school, were gathered in the living room waiting to hear Fenn's story. His mother, with the help of his sisters, had put on a big feast in celebration of his visit home. The dishes were done and the children were playing in a nearby room.

Yesterday afternoon when Willie and Andy came home from school and found their big brother there, they pounced on him, and wrestled with him. Excited, they pestered him to tell them all about the beautiful Dilladora Dobson. Fenn, wanting to tell his curious family the story only one time, put them off until they could all hear it at once.

"Ah...come on Fenn, get on with the story. We've waited long enough," complained Willie.

"Begin at the beginning," his mother, May Dunley Dinkle, requested.

"Yes, yes do!" his sisters exclaimed almost simultaneously.

He smiled. "All right." Having practiced on Isadora, it was easier to tell it. However, even a slightly edited version would not suffice for his family, so he resigned himself to a more lengthy account.

His family, always his best audience, began laughing from the onset of the story and did not quit until the end. They *stopped* laughing, however, when he related how he told Isadora he was quitting. Not only did they stop laughing, they protested loudly.

"You mean you're quitting a job that pays you $2000 a week?" asked fifteen-year-old Andy, aghast.

"But Fenn, are you going to move out and never see Dilladora again?" asked his romantic oldest sister, Emmeline.

"That's the plan."

"But," protested Lavinnia, "you seemed to care about the family."

"I do, Lavinnia."

"Why don't you bring Dilly to visit us, Fenn?" his mother suggested eagerly.

"Oh yes, yes," Cecelia agreed with great enthusiasm.

"Why?"

"Because...because we like her," Cecelia admitted.

Fenn's father, Hans Dinkle, chuckled, then Willie piped up in a complaining voice, "I wanted to see Dilladora do her jujitsu on some bad guy."

They all laughed. As they quieted down, they heard the children in the next room crying and one came in telling on the other, signaling to the parents that it was time to take them home and put them to bed.

# Chapter Twenty-Three

Early Friday morning, driving back to Bostonville, Fenn felt revived and renewed by his family.

He needed to get back and search for a job and he didn't look forward to it. Trying to start his own publishing company now—was premature. The investments he'd made after the sale of his software company were doing well and he preferred keeping them intact a while longer. He was sure that Isadora's promise to help him get started with his goal was now null and void. If only he could have kept working for her at least six months, he might have had enough to actively pursue his goal.

How soon would Isadora hire another bodyguard? he wondered. For the last couple of days, a feeling of uneasiness, over her hiring someone else, had hovered around the edges of his consciousness. Now it pummeled him full force right in the stomach, so to speak. Reminding himself, this time out loud, "Dilly will be safer with some one other than myself, that is, if the next bodyguard doesn't inspire a contest of wills."

Fenn's thoughts reverted to yesterday, wondering how the day went for Dilly. He looked at his watch. Right now she and Isadora were probably having breakfast together. More than once he found himself missing the fiery Dilladora Dobson, as he was at this very moment. The absurdity of it made him chuckle, feeling certain that it would pass after Isadora hired a trustworthy man to take his place.

~~~~~~~~~~~~

Dilladora boarded the bus ready to start the day, but not looking forward to it. Reflecting upon this phenomenon, she realized the cause of it. Fenn! She smiled at herself. Fenn was like none of the other bodyguards—or like no other man she knew, for that matter. His agile mind had trapped her more than once. Outwitting him added much excitement to her life and not once had she succeeded! And now the opportunity to beat him had been rudely snatched away from her—by Fenn himself.

"Oh well," she muttered to herself, "I'll get my zip back once he's out of my life for good."

~~~~~~~~~~

Arriving at his apartment around 10:00 A.M., Fenn deposited his small suit case in the bedroom, and immediately went back downstairs to see Isadora. He went straight to the library and looked in. He was shocked. She was there all right, but apparently already interviewing someone to take his place! He had turned to leave when Isadora called to him.

"Fenn, you're back!" she exclaimed. "Do come in, I want you to meet this young man."

Fenn walked over to them. "Hello, Isadora."

"Fenn, this is George Pappioni, a new applicant for the bodyguard position. Mr. Pappioni, this is Fenn Dinkle."

"Glad ta meetcha," replied George.

"Sit down, Fenn, I would like to have you stay for the interview. Mr. Pappioni has just arrived."

Fenn obliged her and sat. As the interview progressed, irritation stirred inside him, but by the time the interview ended, the irritation had turned into full blown agitation.

After Isadora saw George to the door, application in hand she walked back into the library only to find Fenn pacing the floor. Upon seeing her, he blurted out, "I don't like him."

"Why, Fenn, you don't know him."

"I don't mean I don't like *him*, I mean I don't like him for the job."

"Can we know that without reviewing the application?"

"Yes we can. He hasn't developed his mind, just his muscles."

"We can be sure then," she pointed out, "that he won't challenge Dilly."

"But there's a happy medium, Isadora," Fenn stated firmly. "The man you hire has to be somewhat alert and aware of danger. George wouldn't know danger if it bloodied his nose."

Isadora chuckled. "You're probably right. Would you do me a favor, Fenn?"

"If I can."

"Sit down."

"Oh." Taking stock of his behavior, he smiled. "I will, thanks."

"I need another favor. I would like you to stay on for one more week—just to help me decide who to hire."

"I would like to help you out, Isadora, but I need to look for a job."

"There will be time for you to do that in between interviews. In the meantime, you can remain in the apartment and still collect the same salary."

"It sounds tempting since I don't have another place to live. As you know, rentals are scarce here in Bostonville."

"All right then, you'll consent to do this?"

"Yes, but only for one week. Dilly isn't going to appreciate me staying on. In fact, I had better fix my own meals".

"Sophie may get her feelings hurt over that, Fenn."

Mulling that over a moment, he said, "I'm afraid you're right." He shook his head ruefully. "Then I'll eat earlier or later than you and Dilly."

"Fenn, you are a strong-headed young man. I want you to eat with *us*. I have come to enjoy your company."

"You have?" A slow smile spread across his face. "Well, I'll have to confess, I've had some distress contemplating not being able to enjoy yours and Dilly's company in the future—and Max and Sophie's too."

"Then it's settled. I have another applicant coming in this afternoon at two."

~~~~~~~~~~~~

After the second applicant left, Fenn was even more distressed.

"Well?" asked Isadora.

"I don't like him."

Isadora laughed. "Is this going to be your stock answer?"

"But I mean it this time, Isadora, I don't like *him*. There is something a little devious about him. Call it—a hunch."

Isadora was thoughtful. "Well—I've come to respect your hunches, Fenn. He's a definite no, then."

# Chapter Twenty-Four

It was a lovely, balmy evening. The recent rain had made everything greener and the flowers were blooming profusely. The late afternoon sun gave off a mellow warmth as Fenn waited on the veranda for dinner. Leaning back in the chair, he clasped his hands behind his head and stretched out his long legs. He sighed, realizing that he was also going to miss this beautiful back yard.

"Good evening, Fenn," Isadora said, sitting at the table. She glanced at her watch. "Dilly should be walking in the front door any minute."

Five minutes later, Dilly stepped out onto the veranda from the hallway and stopped in her tracks.

"Dunley!"

"Dillweed." He gave her a pleasant-afternoon-type look.

"How come *he* is still here, Aunt Issy?"

"Why ask me?" rejoined her aunt, innocently.

"Why are you still here, Dunley? Still sticking like crazy glue?"

"You bet. There is no one I would rather stick to than you—since you look so nice tonight."

She put her hands upon her hips. "Did you hear that, Aunt Issy? All he does anymore is spew out flattery."

"Compliments," he corrected.

"Same difference."

"Sit down, Dilladora," said her aunt. "I feel like you're hovering."

Dilly sat down. "When will you be leaving, Dunley?"

"Wel-ll," he drawled, "I kinda like it here, Dillweed. The lodging is good, the food is great and the company is even better."

Dilly, frowning and totally puzzled, opened her mouth to speak just as Sophie, beaming from ear to ear, wheeled out a cart of wonderful looking food.

"Well! It's good to see you cheerful again, Sophie," remarked Dilly, a sarcastic edge to her voice. "You've been all gloom and doom for the past two days."

"Did you miss me, Sophie?" asked Fenn, grinning.

"I did, Mr. Fenn."

"Good, because I missed you *and* your cooking. In fact, I bragged so much about your cooking, I think my mother was a bit jealous."

"Oh, go on with you," Sophie replied, smiling broadly.

"How was your visit home, Fenn?" asked Isadora.

"It was great. In fact my mother and sisters provided a big feast in honor of my visit."

"That was nice," remarked Isadora.

"How did they all react to you being a quitter, Dunley?"

"Interesting question, Dillweed. Andy, my fifteen-year-old brother was aghast that I would even think of giving up such a salary."

"And the others?" pursued Dilly.

"Well first, I have to tell you that before I told them I had quit, I entertained them with stories about guarding the beautiful Dilladora Dobson."

"You did?" questioned Dilly, shocked. A small pout formed around her mouth. "I don't think I like that."

"Like it or not, Dilladora Dobson, the stories belong to me as well as you."

Internalizing his statement, Dilly was silent for some time and then in a small voice she asked, "And how did they react to the stories?"

"They rolled on the floor with laughter, so to speak. Then I told them I quit and they all fell apart—except my father and he just chuckled over everyone's reactions."

"What do you mean, they all fell apart?" queried Dilly, curiosity still getting the best of her.

"Well, let me think—Emmeline , my oldest sister was concerned about me moving out and never seeing you again. Lavinnia was concerned that I would miss the whole family. My mother wanted me to bring you down there for a visit and Cecelia seconded the motion with great enthusiasm."

"Why?" asked Dilly, incredulous.

Fenn grinned. "That's what I asked." He stopped to sneak in a bite of food that was getting cold.

"Why?" insisted Dilly.

Swallowing the mouthful, he answered, "Let me see, she said, and I quote: 'Because we like her.'"

"She really said that?" asked Dilly.

"Yes. Unbelievable, huh?" His eyes were teasing. "But then, my family is a little kooky. And," he continued, "Willie, my thirteen-year-old brother was more disappointed than all of them. He wanted to see you topple a bad guy into a heap on the floor."

Dilly laughed, then just as suddenly became silent, and remained so for the rest of the meal, allowing Fenn to eat in peace. The only interruption was a polite question now and then from Isadora. It was always a little hard to eat the food while it was still warm when dining with these two.

When they were enjoying Sophie's dessert of berry cobbler, Fenn asked, "Are you going out tonight, Dilly?"

"I don't have to answer that."

"If you recall, you never had to. But you can tell me now as I won't be following and interfering in your life anymore."

"To my relief," she asserted, trying hard to match her feelings to the words.

"And mine," Fenn said. But underneath, he felt a little unnerved not knowing—used to finding out one way or another where Dilly was going and with whom.

# Chapter Twenty-Five

Monday, Isadora resumed interviewing new applicants. Fenn had spent all day Saturday checking out job opportunities. After church on Sunday, he spent all afternoon looking for a new apartment, but to no avail. He couldn't tell if this had anything to do with his dour mood this morning. He suspected that more than likely it was the thought of having to help Isadora interview all the job applicants. She had scheduled interviews for the next four days straight. Added to this, living in such proximity to Dilly and not knowing what she was up to, was becoming more unnerving each day. Divesting himself of the responsibility of protecting her was proving more difficult than he expected.

~~~~~~~~~~~~

Thursday afternoon of the fourth day, the interviews were winding down. Isadora and Fenn had just finished interviewing the eighth candidate and were visiting in the library.

"Well, Fenn, what is your verdict on this last one?"

Fenn was silent so long, Isadora added, "Since you've vetoed all seven of the others, we need to think more carefully about this last one."

"He's passable I guess," Fenn mumbled.

"All right then, I think I'll hire him."

Ignoring her decision, he asked, "Isadora, where did you get this passel of clowns?"

"I got them from three different weight training centers in Bostonville and Medford City."

"Weight training centers? You know as well as I do, Isadora, all you get in weight training centers, are a bunch of muscle-bound light-weights."

"But," Isadora pointed out gently, "that's where I got you."

"Yes...I know...but...well, you got to know me fairly well before you asked me to interview. How well do you know any of these candidates?"

"Not well."

"How can you even consider them, then?"

"You quit so suddenly, Fenn, I had no choice."

Fenn was silent for some moments, thinking, then he said, almost under his breath, "This bodyguard business is just plain foolishness—idiocy ."

"Why, Fenn?"

He got up and began pacing. "Dang it, Isadora, this girl needs a *husband*, not a bodyguard."

"I know that, Fenn, but what can I do about it?"

"Interview applicants!" He stopped pacing and stared at Isadora, realizing the absurdity of his statement. They both laughed.

"You can't imagine how often I've wished that I could 'arrange' a marriage for Dilly."

He sat down. "Why isn't she married? She certainly has enough men after her."

"For the same reason you aren't. The right one hasn't come along. She's certain that she'll never find a man like her Uncle Obadiah, so she's resigned to remaining single."

"It's a shame, Isadora, a downright shame. She would make a wonderful mother. She needs to be raising her own children, not counseling mixed up kids who don't want her help."

"I know."

Fenn stood up abruptly. "Isadora, would you tell Sophie that I won't be home for dinner?"

She hesitated a moment, wanting to ask why, but refrained. "Yes, I will."

"Please, Isadora, don't hire anyone just yet. There is something I have to do tonight."

"All right, Fenn."

Fenn pulled a piece of bun from his second hot dog and tossed it into the pond for the ducks. He loved this park, a beautiful, peaceful place to think, far from the Penbroke household. And that was what he had come here for—to think, to pray, to sort out the myriad thoughts that had been both tantalizing and tormenting him. He had to sort out and understand the emotions these thoughts evoked. Finally, like different sides of a magnet, his emotions pulled him away from and then thrust him back to the inevitable conclusion. The laughter of children playing in the park was music to his ears as the sun went down casting a shimmering glow of orange-red color across the pond.

An hour later, Fenn found himself still sitting on the bank of the pond, watching the reflection of lamp lights dancing upon the water. He knew what he had to do, what he wanted to do, hoping and praying it would turn out the way his anxious heart desired.

~~~~~~~~~~~~~

Isadora closed the library doors as Fenn requested. She walked over and sat across from him, noticing that the agitation was gone and that a demeanor of calm assurance had taken its place.

"We missed you at dinner tonight. I hope you've eaten."

"I have, thank you."

"What is it, Fenn? What did you want to talk to me about?"

"I've found a husband for Dilladora."

Isadora didn't know what to expect, but knew that this most certainly was not it! She pulled back, frowning, "Uh...when did you...how..."

"I've known him for some time, Isadora, and he's very reliable."

Isadora was shocked—dismayed. "Fenn, you can't just choose a husband for Dilly!"

"I can and I have—it's me."

"You?"

"Yes, me. I know I'm being presumptuous to think I could possibly live up to Dilly's idol, Obadiah. Nevertheless, Isadora, I'm asking you for her hand."

Isadora sat very still, staring at Fenn—then she smiled. "Why Fenn, when did you decide that you—wanted to marry Dilly?"

"I don't know for sure. Subconsciously, the day before I quit, I think. Consciously, tonight at the park."

"You haven't known Dilly very long, Fenn, are you sure?"

"I've known her for almost three weeks. And as I said, so much happened during those six days on the job, making it possible to know her in a way I couldn't otherwise."

"How do you propose to support her?"

"I've given that a lot of thought. There are several things I can do which will provide a good living for her—nothing like she's used to, but a good living nevertheless."

"How do you suppose Dilly will react to your intentions?"

The agitation returned, and soon he was up on his feet pacing the floor. "That's the sixty-four-dollar question, Isadora. She is the most stubborn, contrary girl I have ever known! Believe me, I did *not* want to fall in love with her."

"Why do you love her, Fenn?"

"Because she is the most *unique* girl I have ever known. She's unaffected by her beauty, by money and prestige. She is the kindest, the funniest, the most loving, intelligent girl I've ever known—and her morals and values are pure gold."

Isadora's eyes filled with tears. "I give you my consent—and my blessing, Fenn." She paused, smiling, "And—I wish you luck."

# Chapter Twenty-Six

Friday morning was a glorious morning in Fenn's book. He arrived in the dining room, wearing jeans and a big smile.

"Good morning, Dilly. I see you're wearing the same outfit you had on the very first day I saw you. And I might add, those colors do show off your beautiful hair."

Dilly stared, wide eyed in surprise, then squinted in suspicion. "What's up, Dunley?"

"My spirits, that's what," he grinned broadly.

"How long do I have to put up with you, Fenn Dinkle?"

"Wel-ll," he drawled, "that remains to be seen."

Dilly finished filling her plate from the buffet and now ignoring Fenn, headed out to the veranda, just as Isadora entered.

"Good morning, Fenn. How are you feeling this morning?"

"Like I could conquer the world." His eyes sparkled with excitement as he added the finishing touches to his overflowing plate.

"You may just have to do that."

He smiled and nodded in agreement. "Excuse me, Isadora, but I'm going to follow Dilly to the veranda. You are welcome to join us. In fact, I'm sure you'll be the only one welcome out there." He left the dining room and walked through the kitchen.

Fenn put his plate on the table and sat down. "May I join you, Dilly?"

"It looks like you already have. Would it have done any good if I had said no?"

"No," he grinned.

"That's what I thought."

"How did your counseling go on Wednesday?"

"I don't want to discuss it."

"Have you behaved yourself, Dilly, since I quit?"

"No."

"That's what I thought."

Isadora brought her plate and joined them. They all three ate in silence for a while, then Isadora spoke.

"Dilladora and Fenn, I have something to tell you—Hank Judd and his friend have been arrested by the FBI for drug dealing."

Dilly put her fork down and gaped at her aunt, shocked. "Drug dealing—the FBI?"

"Yes."

"That...that means they have been wanted in other states?"

"That's right, Dilladora. Hank Judd is the leader of a large drug ring that the FBI has been trying to get evidence on for years. They finally got the evidence, but he disappeared and changed his name. They were hiding out in Bostonville and were running their sleazy business from here." Next, Isadora surprised even Fenn. "My friend, Lt. Billings from the Bostonville Police department has been working with the FBI. He's coming here this afternoon to ask you both some questions. You will have to cancel your modeling session, Dilly. He's coming around 2:00."

"Bernie will be furious with me," Dilly said, speaking mostly to herself.

"Nevertheless, Dilladora, you have to be here, you have no choice. By the way, Fenn, I want to thank you."

"Fenn?" questioned Dilly, stilled dazed. "What did he do?"

Isadora related the story to Dilly, telling her of Fenn's role in apprehending their would-be litigators/drug dealers.

Dilly's appetite suddenly disappeared. "Aunt Isadora, I'm sorry...I was so stupid. It scares me to think what would have happened if...if Fenn hadn't been along and if he hadn't grabbed that video." She gazed at Fenn a moment. "I guess you are the hero of the day, Dunley," she conceded a little wanly. "How...uh..." she swallowed more humble pie, "how can I thank you?"

"By giving me a few minutes of your time tonight after dinner, at 7:00 in the library."

"I uh...I have an engagement tonight at 8:00."

"That's fine, I'll be through before then. I would like you to be there too, Isadora, if you will."

"Me?" she asked, surprised.

"Yes."

"All right, I'll be there."

"Will you two excuse me?" Dilly requested, getting up. "I'm afraid I can't eat another bite."

They both watched Dilly disappear into the kitchen.

"I've never seen Dilly quite so contrite," remarked Fenn.

"Let's hope it lasts. What are you up to, Fenn?"

"I don't know if what I'm going to do will backfire on me or not, but this I do know, Isadora, Dilly is such an unusual girl, the 'usual' wouldn't catch her attention or—might not work with her."

"Well," she smiled, "I'll be on pins and needles 'till 7:00 tonight."

"Me too," he said. "Will you excuse me, Isadora? I have several errands to run today."

Fenn walked into the kitchen with his empty plate and saw Max and Sophie enjoying breakfast together.

"You are just the two I want to see. Are you both going to be around tonight at 7:00?"

"Why, I believe we are, aren't we, Sophie?"

She nodded. "What's up, Mr. Fenn?"

"Something downright scary, Sophie, and I need you in my corner. Would you both be in the library at 7:00 tonight?"

"We'll be there for sure," she said with conviction.

"Thanks, Sophie," he said leaning down and kissing her on the cheek. "Thanks, Max."

~~~~~~~~~~~~

"Good afternoon, John," greeted Isadora as she opened the front door. "Come in, my niece and Fenn Dinkle are waiting for you in the library."

The tall gray-haired man smiled as he stepped inside. "Thank you, Isadora. It's good to see you."

As they entered the library, Isadora introduced them. "Dilly and Fenn, I would like you to meet Lt. John Billings; John, this is my niece Dilly Dobson; and Fenn Dinkle, the one who has managed to rescue us from what could have been a very serious situation."

"More serious than you know, Isadora," added John Billings.

"More serious?" Fear clutched at her heart. "What is it John?"

"I'll tell you all as soon as I ask a few questions."

"Please have a seat, John," Isadora said, indicating with her hand one of the sofas in front of the fireplace. Isadora sat on one end, while he sat on the other. Dilly and Fenn seated themselves upon the facing sofa.

Lt. Billings addressed Dilly. "We have arrested your friend, Gloria Bradford."

Dilly paled. "You...you arrested Gloria? Whatever for?"

"I'll explain after you answer some questions. How long have you known Gloria?"

"Let me think...I met her in my second year of college. I have known her for approximately five years."

"How did you meet her?"

"In a history class we had together. We took many of the same classes since we were both majoring in History."

"Did she graduate with you?"

"No, she dropped out of college after about a year-and-a-half. Her parents were supporting her and they were having financial problems. She decided to work for a year."

"Did you keep in touch with her?"

"No, she kept in touch with me. She would call every once in a while and ask if we could have lunch together."

"Did you?"

"Once in a while."

"What did you talk about when you had lunch together?"

"She always wanted to talk about her problems. Apparently, she couldn't talk to her parents."

"What were her problems?"

"Boyfriend problems...or to be accurate, the lack of them."

"Any other problems?" prodded the Lieutenant.

Dilly thought a minute. "Well, she was always in a bind financially. She didn't seem to manage money well."

"How did you meet Hank Judd?"

"Several weeks ago, Gloria called and insisted I meet her for lunch. She wanted me to meet a man she was interested in. I met her at the Cherry Street Tea Room and she introduced me to her friend, Clay Humphrey, and then introduced Hank Judd as Clay's close friend."

"When did Hank Judd ask you out?"

"The next day. He wanted us to double with Gloria and Clay."

"Did you accept?"

"No. He made my skin crawl." Dilly heard an intake of breath from her aunt and felt Fenn's eyes on her. Not acknowledging either one, she stared straight ahead at Lt. Billings. "A little later that same evening, Gloria called and begged me to go out with them, explaining that Clay was a little shy about going out with her alone and she wanted Clay to feel comfortable. I told her that Clay didn't seem shy to me, but she insisted that it was because Hank was there. I told her again that I didn't want to go out with Hank. She started to cry and said that this was the first man in a long time that seemed interested in her. I felt sorry for her, so finally I said I would go, but told her that this would be the last time."

The Lieutenant was silent a moment, then he said, his face serious, "and it might have been your last time, literally, if this young man here hadn't foiled the kidnapping."

"Kidnapping!" Dilly and Isadora exclaimed together.

Fenn felt the blood drain from his face.

"Yes. After we and the FBI arrested Hank Judd and Clay Humphrey, they squealed on your so-called friend. By the way, those names are aliases. Apparently they met Gloria in a bar one night. They learned in short order that she took drugs and decided to use that knowledge to their advantage. Since they were hiding out, a good deal of their funds were not readily available at the moment. They promised Gloria free drugs and a lot of money if she could come up with an idea for all three of them to make some quick money—say a little harmless kidnapping maybe. Immediately, she recalled you telling her of your fake kidnapping and informed them of the wealth of the Penbroke family. When we arrested Gloria, she denied everything, but she soon broke because she needed drugs."

"Thank you for being so cooperative, Dilly. I had to get some answers from you in order to put together a few missing pieces of the puzzle. Well—I think that's about it as far as my questions are concerned. Do any of you have questions?"

"But how were they intending to pull it off?" Fenn blurted out. "Dilly isn't the easiest girl to kidnap!"

Lt. Billings smiled. "So I've heard from several sources and especially from those two scum who have been squawking over their injuries. They're in a rage at Gloria Bradford for choosing, and I give you a *very* edited quote: 'that damned, (blankety-blankety-blank) unmanageable redhead.' They can't believe that after skirting the law successfully for years, they got busted because of her. And, to give you another *very* edited quote: 'that stupid, long-legged, (blankety-blankety-blank) dumb-luck jerk.'"

Isadora would have smiled at the quotes if she weren't feeling so frightened over what could have happened. She studied her niece, "Did you suspect anything at all that night, Dilly?"

"Yes."

"You did?" Fenn asked, surprised. Suddenly angry, he burst out, "Why in the heck didn't you tell me?!"

"You were already too angry. Besides—I began to wonder if it was my imagination."

"What was it, Dilly?" questioned the lieutenant. "Maybe I can help you out."

"We all had drinks before we started watching the video. They had cocktails. I had a root beer, which tasted odd, but what I felt was more odd was the way Gloria watched me. She seemed very nervous, and only when I took another small sip of the root beer did she relax a little. I began to feel suspicious and just held the drink. Gloria got nervous again and asked me if I was going to drink the root beer. I noticed Hank Judd glare at her. It was then that I decided to find a way to get out of there and down to the parking lot where Fenn was. I told Gloria I wasn't thirsty, right then, but that I would drink it later while we were watching the video. Immediately, Hank put the video in and we began watching it. After a while, when an unsavory scene appeared, I used it to cause the ruckus with the video. I wanted Hank to get angry so I would have an excuse to leave. I didn't realize it was going to get quite so out of hand."

"It wasn't your imagination, Dilly," Lt. Billings interjected. "Hank Judd, knowing he had nothing more to lose, told us everything in order to get back at Gloria. Your root beer had knockout drops in it. When you were out, they were going to carry you down the hall to a vacant apartment that they had also rented when they first moved to

Bostonville. They rented it under another alias in case they had to hide out again. The plan was to keep you blindfolded, gagged and tied until it was over. Fenn following you up to the apartment put a monkey wrench into their plans. The time before last when Gloria talked to you, Dilly, you didn't have a bodyguard, so it threw them when Fenn showed up. But they decided to go ahead with it. Their revised plan was for Gloria to run down to the parking lot and try to find Fenn and ask if he'd seen Dilly, then tell him that she got angry and left. Gloria was going to act very upset about it, then ask him to drive her home.

There are a few more details they worked out, but that's about the gist of it. The lawsuit was an afterthought since the other plan fell through. And in their minds, it was a slower but an easier way to come by some funds." Lt. Billings chuckled. "I think that Hank and Clay should have stayed with just selling drugs, they were better at it than kidnapping."

Dilly was visibly shaken but managed a reply. "Thank you, Lt. Billings for telling us the details. I'm grateful that we are all safe— but—I feel bad for Gloria. Are her folks standing behind her?"

"I think so. They came down to visit her and have hired a lawyer. Well, folks," he said, standing up, "I must get back down to the station and finish up the report." He held out his hand to Fenn, who was also on his feet, and shook his hand firmly. "That was good detective work, son, thanks." Then he put his hand on Dilly's shoulder. "And you, young lady, were very astute and quick thinking. Dilly, Fenn," he said, smiling at each, "any time you decide to join me in law enforcement, I'd be glad to have you. You're quite a team."

Fenn smiled at this. "Thank you, sir. I think we are a good team." His heart skipped a beat as he thought of tonight's appointment with Dilly.

They all walked to the front door with Lt. Billings and said good-bye. As the door shut, the three looked at each other, their hearts still beating faster than normal. Isadora broke the silence.

"I think I'm going upstairs and lie down for a while. Will you both excuse me? I'll see you at dinner."

There was a look of concern on Dilly's face as she watched her aunt walk slowly upstairs. She turned to Fenn. Her head high, she tried to sound snippy, "Well, are you going to tell me 'I told you so?'"

He gazed down at her. The expression in his eyes unsettled her, causing her heart to pound and the blood rush to her face. Her question burst out on a flutter of breath, "Well?"

A faint smile appeared on his lips, his eyes holding hers, he answered slowly, "No, I'm going to tell you that I have some errands to run, and that I won't be home for dinner, but—I'll be here for our appointment tonight."

~~~~~~~~~

Isadora, Dilly, Max and Sophie were in the library promptly at 7:00 P.M., looking at each other, puzzled and curious. If Isadora was slightly less puzzled than the others, she refrained from commenting.

Fenn, the man of the hour, arrived at 7:05. His light beige pants were neatly pressed as was his deep maroon linen shirt. His shiny blonde hair was neatly combed. And his hazel eyes were alight with excitement, matching the smile that spread across his face.

"Good evening, everyone. I'm glad you could all be here. Dilly, you look especially lovely tonight. Who is the lucky man?"

"You don't know him, Dunley," she was quick to answer.

"I assume he's trustworthy?" he teased.

"No, he's a scoundrel."

"Well—now that brings me to the subject of our meeting tonight," he said, beginning to pace back and forth in front of the fireplace.

Max and Sophie were sitting on one of the sofas, Dilly and Isadora on the other, and the four pairs of eyes followed him as he paced. Finally, he stopped directly in front of the fireplace and spoke.

"Dilly, I don't think you should allow your aunt to choose your bodyguards anymore. I think *you* should choose the next one."

Dilly's mouth dropped open, then she looked over at her aunt questioningly, then at Max and Sophie. All three shrugged their shoulders.

"Well, of all the audacity, Fenn Dinkle."

"I know," he agreed. "Did you know that this week, while you were at school, your aunt and I have interviewed eight muscle-headed applicants for the job of bodyguard?"

"No! Aunt Issy how could you? I told you I would do better, that I didn't need a bodyguard anymore."

"Nevertheless," Fenn spoke up before Isadora could, "we did interview and *I* vetoed them all."

"Ooh! Of all the pompous nerve," Dilly almost screeched as she stood up. Isadora, grabbing hold of her skirt, pulled her back down on the couch. Dilly stared at her aunt in shock. "Aunt Issy!"

"Hear him out, Dilladora."

Fenn, unruffled by the incident, continued. "Let me tell you why I vetoed them, Dilly. I vetoed them because none of them could protect you like you deserve to be protected."

"Oh? And who do you suppose could do that, Fenn Dinkle?"

"I think *you* should take the applications, not your aunt—and *I* would like to be the first applicant."

He picked up a paper from the fireplace mantle and handed it to her.

"But you quit, and I don't want a..." Her voice trailed off as she looked at the heading of the application.

"APPLICATION FOR A LIFETIME BODYGUARD"

She scrutinized it then looked up at Fenn. "What...what does 'Application For a Lifetime Bodyguard' mean?"

Sophie's eyes got big and her mouth dropped open as she looked across at Isadora—who was smiling.

"It means, Dilladora, that I'm applying for it for life, because no one will protect you like *I* will and besides—I can't stand the thought of anyone trying to take care of you but—me."

"Aunt Issy?" she squeaked, panic in her voice.

"Don't look at me, Dilladora, you're on your own."

Her eyebrows knitted together in apprehension. Her eyes, begging to be extricated, looked over at Isadora, at Sophie and Max, then back to Fenn—who rescued her.

"You don't have to accept or reject my application right now, Dilly." Fenn looked at each one. "I appreciate all of you being here— especially Dilly. His eyes lingered on hers. Now would you, Isadora, Sophie and Max mind if I have a moment alone with Dilly?"

Dilly opened her mouth to protest but Isadora and Sophie agreed so vocally and eagerly, she didn't have a chance. The three left quickly, shutting the doors behind them.

"Dilly, I want you to think about my application tonight and I would like to talk to you about it after breakfast tomorrow morning," he said, stepping around behind one of the sofas and picking up one red rose in a crystal stem vase from behind an antique brass lamp. He walked back around to Dilly and sat next to her.

Taking a careful breath, he gazed into her beautiful blue eyes—which were wide with shock—and gave her the rose. "I love you, Dilladora Dobson," he said, softly. "I love you."

She stared at him—for once totally speechless.

"Though I wouldn't admit it to myself, I was intrigued with you the first day on the job, from that moment on the bus when you gave the seat offered you—to the young mother with the baby—then when you shoved your elbow into the stomach of the leering man who offered it." He smiled. "I think that was the beginning of my downfall and I've been falling ever since—in love, that is." Noting that she was still in a state of shock, he continued.

"I've dated many young women in my life, Dilly, and I've never met a girl like you, one as unique, as kind, as comical," he grinned and added, "as stubborn, as difficult," then his face became serious, "as loving and—as wonderful."

Dilly's eyes were wide and wondering. Fenn stood up, leaned over and took hold of her arms, pulling her up. He searched her face for some encouragement no matter how small, but before she could say anything, he couldn't resist kissing her delectable lips—tenderly, quickly.

His heart beating wildly, he spoke breathlessly, "It's almost time to leave for your date, Dilly. I hope you will at least consider letting us now get acquainted under different circumstances. Please, my darling Dilly, give me a chance to show you what a good lifetime bodyguard I'll be." With great effort, he dropped his hands, releasing her.

The pulse in her neck throbbing noticeably, Dilly turned and walked—as if hypnotized—slowly and mechanically toward the door, rose in one hand and application in the other. Turning, she gazed at Fenn, took a few more steps, turned and gazed at him again then crossed the hall and moved slowly up the stairs until she was out of sight.

His heart pounding, Fenn collapsed onto the sofa, sweating profusely.

# Chapter Twenty-Seven

Fenn tossed and turned during the hours before midnight, reliving his proposal to Dilly then fell into a deep and exhausted sleep. He awoke with the same feeling of excitement he had as a youngster on Christmas morning—at the same time nervous as a boy going out on his first date.

After showering, he felt somewhat calmer and more self-assured. By the time he'd shaved, put on a pair of jeans and a casual shirt, it was time for breakfast.

He found Sophie arranging a big bouquet of flowers on the veranda table. On the cart was a plate of fruit and another plate of homemade cinnamon rolls. Picking up a pitcher of orange juice and another one of milk, she placed them on the table.

"Good morning, Sophie."

"Oh, good morning, Mr. Fenn." She returned his smile, her eyes twinkling with happiness.

He sat at the table. "That breakfast looks like a special treat, Sophie."

"Good morning, Fenn," Isadora said, coming out of the hall door.

He beamed. "Good morning, Isadora."

"What a beautiful bouquet, Sophie," remarked Isadora.

"It's in celebration of Mr. Fenn's application to Dilly."

Fenn, pleased, grinned and thanked her.

"Oh, by the way," Sophie said, "Dilly had breakfast a little earlier."

"Oh?" Fenn's face fell. "How...how did she seem, Sophie?"

"Well, I would say...a little subdued."

"Oh? What do you suppose that means, Isadora?"

"I don't know, Fenn."

"Did she say anything to you last night?"

"Not a word."

"Hmm. You know, Isadora and Sophie, I'm...I'm scared. Dilly is so darn unpredictable."

"We know, Fenn, we know," Isadora said, shaking her head.

When they were through with breakfast, Fenn made a request. "Isadora, would you mind going up to Dilly's room and telling her I would like to speak with her?"

"I wouldn't mind at all."

Fenn followed Isadora, and waited at the bottom of the stairs. Sophie, who had followed them into the foyer, remained a few feet behind. Isadora soon came down stairs.

"She'll be down in a minute, Fenn," she said as she stationed herself next to Sophie.

Presently, Dilly appeared at the top of the stairs looking gorgeous in a pair of jeans and a white shirt.

Fenn, his heart catapulting against his chest, impulsively knelt. "Oh Princess Dillweed, please let down the drawbridge."

Startled, Dilly gazed down at him—then giggled.

"Please, beautiful Princess, I'm drowning in the dark mote! I came to rescue you and if I can't, I fear I will forever be lost."

She giggled again. "Just a moment, Prince Dunley," she said and disappeared into her room. Soon she returned with something in her hand and sat down on the top stair. "Why should I let down the drawbridge, Prince Dunley?" she asked as she worked with 'the something' in her lap.

"Because I've been searching for you for many years, and now that I've finally found you, I see you are a prisoner in a dark castle and I desperately want to rescue you."

Isadora and Sophie looked at each other and shook their heads, both wondering if Fenn and Dilly had taken leave of their senses.

"But why should I let *you* rescue me?" she asked, a saucy look upon her face.

"Because I *love* you. I know I can't hold a candle to the great King Obadiah, Princess Dillweed, but I will love you forever."

"Oh, but Prince Dunley," her smile was radiant, "don't sell yourself short. The only one who could make me laugh until my nose runs, besides the great King Obadiah, is you."

Prince Dunley laughed. "That makes me very happy, Princess Dillweed. If you'll let the drawbridge down so that I can court you, I will supply you with white hankies forever."

Princess Dillweed laughed. "All right Prince Dunley, here is the drawbridge." She held up a flag of a truce: a long pencil from which hung white, washed and *pressed* hankies all tied together by opposite corners.

Prince Dunley was stunned. "You washed and ironed all those hankies, Princess Dillweed?"

"I did, Prince Dunley," she said softly, waving the flag and smiling.

Fenn was sure that his heart had missed a beat or two. For this to happen to him, it seemed unbelievable. He couldn't speak. He could only pull out one of his own new, white hankies and wave it joyfully in her direction.

Dropping her flag, Princess Dillweed ran down to him.

Neither one noticed that Isadora and Sophie had quietly slipped away.

They stood—looking at each other. The aura of magic they had created surrounded them and caught them up in an enchanted moment that excluded the world. He reached out slowly and with infinite tenderness, took her face into his hands and gazed into her gorgeous blue eyes. "I want to take you to meet my family."

"I'd like that," she said, her voice husky with emotion. "I've already fallen in love with your family."

"You have?" His eyes were alight with happiness. "Well, that is a *start*," he said, then still holding her face in his hands, he kissed her forehead, kissed the tip of her lovely nose and then, putting his arms around her, finally kissed her waiting lips.

Dilly threw her arms about his neck and returned his kiss with all the pent up fire and passion of her redheaded nature. A trembling emotion rose from deep inside her, leaving her weak. She drew back, looking with absolute trust into Fenn's eyes, and knew that she was ready at last to open herself to all the love she saw there.

# Chapter Twenty-Eight

Fenn called his family, informing them of his and Dilly's forth-coming visit this very Saturday, and as he expected, their response was more than enthusiastic.

Placing his bag in the car, he drove around the front and parked, ready to go. He waited for Dilly at the foot of the stairs.

Dilly came running down, an overnight case in her hand, dressed in a delightful summer dress.

"I'm ready, Fenn," she said as she looked up at him and smiled— and a glorious smile it was—in Fenn's book.

"Fenn? You are calling me *Fenn* now?" He smiled as his eyes devoured her lovely face.

Isadora came down stairs to say goodbye to the pair and Sophie and Max walked out from the kitchen to bid them a bon voyage.

Dilly, her eyes alive with happiness, kissed Sophie and Max good-bye, then hugged and kissed her aunt Isadora. Fenn followed suit. He kissed Sophie on the cheek, then shook Max's hand affectionately. When he came to Isadora, he bent down and kissed her on the cheek for the first time, then whispered in her ear. "Thank you, Isadora, for giving your consent."

Fenn took Dilly's bag in one hand and took her hand in the other as they stepped to the front door. They both turned and smiled at the 'three doting parents,' then opened the door and went out.

Isadora, Sophie and Max walked quickly into the front room. Looking out the window they watched as Fenn opened the trunk and placed Dilly's suitcase inside. He stopped, looked down at Dilly, then bent down and kissed her once more upon the forehead. She looked up at him, her smile radiant—filled with promise. Fenn then took her by the arm, led her around to the passenger's side and opened the door for her. Walking around to his side, he got in. Looking up at the brown-stone, he glimpsed the three watching through the window. He smiled at them, waved, and drove off.

Sophie spoke first. "When you said you were going to kill two birds with one stone, hire a bodyguard and find her a husband, Issy Mum, I thought you had gone plum loco. Then when you found Mr. Fenn and we saw the fireworks between the two, I just threw up my hands." Max chuckled and Isadora smiled knowingly. "Never thought you could pull it off, Issy Mum, never thought you could pull it off." She fished around in her pocket and pulled out a ten-dollar bill. "You won the bet," she said grinning broadly.

Isadora smiled and took it. "I'll have to admit, Sophie, I was beginning to think *you* were going to win. I couldn't find a young man worthy of Dilly. As you know, to keep Dilly from getting suspicious, I only hired men she couldn't possibly be interested in. But—as time went on, I couldn't find any other kind—until I noticed Fenn. As I got acquainted with him at the center, I was almost positive I had found the young man for her—but he had to prove himself. And prove himself he did—from the very first day."

"He did," Sophie agreed, "but that girl gave him a run for his money and I thought sure we were going to lose him."

"Here's the ten dollars, Sophie," Isadora said, handing it back. "They aren't married yet."

"Oh, but they will be, I'm certain of that."

Isadora thought about it a moment. "I'm certain of it too, Sophie," she said, smiling, and snatching back the bill. "And—I bet you another ten dollars, it won't be very long either."

"No way am I going to take that bet, Issy Mum. No ma'am, I'd lose again."

"Smart girl, Sophie," Max said, grinning. Now, how about the three of us going out to the veranda and celebrating with a tall cold glass of lemonade?"

"Sounds good, Max, Sophie, let's do it!"

Seated on the veranda, lemonade in hand, Isadora smiled fondly at Sophie and Max, then sighed happily. "As the poet Robert Browning said:

'God's in His heaven—
All's right with the world!'"